THE UNNAMABLE

EIMEAR MCBRIDE studied acting at Drama Centre London. Her debut novel *A Girl Is a Half-formed Thing* won the inaugural Goldsmiths Prize, Irish Novel of the Year, the Baileys Women's Prize for Fiction, the Desmond Elliott Prize and the Geoffrey Faber Memorial Prize. Her second novel *The Lesser Bohemians* won the James Tait Black Memorial Prize and was shortlisted for many others; her novel *The City Changes Its Face* was published in 2025. She is the inaugural holder of the Beckett Research Centre's Creative Fellowship at the University of Reading. She writes and reviews for the *Guardian*, *New Statesman* and the *Times Literary Supplement*, and she lives in London.

T0381993

SAMUEL BECKETT

The Unnamable

faber

Originally published as *L'Innommable* in France in 1953
by Les Éditions de Minuit
This English translation, by the author, first published in the USA in 1958
by Grove Press. Collected in *Three Novels*
(Grove Press 1958; Olympia Press 1959)
First published in the UK in 1960 by Calder and Boyars Publishers

This edition first published in 2025
by Faber & Faber Limited
The Bindery, 51 Hatton Garden
London, EC1N 8HN

Printed and bound in Great Britain by CPI Group (UK) Ltd, Croydon, CRO 4YY
Typeset by Typo•glyphix, Burton-on-Trent, DE14 3HE

Note to reader: The Unnamable was first published in English in 1958. The language
in these pages is a reflection of the period in which the book was written.

A CIP record for this book is available from the British Library

ISBN 978-0-571-38674-1

MIX
Paper | Supporting
responsible forestry
FSC® C013604

Printed and bound in the UK on FSC® certified paper in line with our continuing
commitment to ethical business practices, sustainability and the environment.
For further information see faber.co.uk/environmental-policy

Our authorised representative in the EU for product safety is
Easy Access System Europe, Mustamäe tee 50, 10621 Tallinn, Estonia
gpsr.requests@easproject.com

2 4 6 8 10 9 7 5 3

FOREWORD

by Eimear McBride

Perversely, considering the novel's refusal to stop, *The Unnamable* arrived at the end of a beginning for Beckett, or of a second beginning anyway. Having commenced his scratchings under the influence of Joyce's literature of accumulation – and toiled in the trenches of the unpublished as a result – Beckett was overdue his own great 'revelation' by its advent in 1946. Fictionally memorialised as occurring on Dún Laoghaire's East Pier, in *Krapp's Last Tape*, Beckett's actual Damascene moment occurred in his mother's room when it suddenly became clear to him that Joyce's technique was proving more hobble than help. That reaching deeply into his own sense of ignorance, impotence, folly and repression was the grist his mill required instead. This reversion to a literature of diminishment, and peeling away, led to Beckett's most prolific phase, the so-called 'siege in the room' which spawned *The End*, *Mercier and Camier*, *Waiting for Godot*, *Molloy*, *Malone Dies* and *The Unnamable*. Each was originally written in French – all the better to prevent the richness of Irish English infecting his new linguistic impoverishment with any trace of the dreaded 'style'.

So, from the revelation on, it was plot, character and even the vaguest nod to social realism, begone! While he may not have shed all these elements at once by the time he got as far as *The Unnamable,* in 1953, his prose had been stripped to the bone and the bone itself boiled white. Never again were the literary curlicues of reasoning or plausibility to be indulged in, while even time and place – the basic security blankets of novelists everywhere – were thenceforth made redundant. With this massacre of critical expectation complete, *The Unnamable*'s sole remaining vehicle was voice and, in finding it, the writer arrived at his ultimate form. In the 1960s, Beckett is said to have exclaimed to the poet, John Montague, who was just then struggling with the structure of a particular poem, 'Ah, Montague, what you need is monologue – *monologue!* That's the thing.' And monologue is certainly the easiest feature of *The Unnamable* to identify but, after that, it gets a lot murkier.

Explicitly – or as explicit as it's possible to be when characterising a voice which rejects its own definition – *The Unnamable* is the monologue of an unnamed, monodical being who is, seemingly, forever compelled forwards by the imperative of its unverifiable, yet unfortunately un-discontinuable, and un-silenceable, existence. Or, as he says himself, 'Ah if only this voice could stop, this meaningless voice which prevents you from being nothing.'

What can be gleaned, thanks to his fixatious reiteration of various preoccupations – although one shouldn't be foolish enough to believe these assertions signal any objective truth – is that 'he', for want of a name, has always been there or if he hasn't he can't remember where else he might have been before. There was a mother: 'I am looking for my mother to kill her.' A place of birth: 'Bally I forget what'. And intimations of God denied: 'Yes, God, fomenter of calm, I never believed, not a second.' He says he lives in a jar, sometimes beneath a tarpaulin, with his hands on his knees, or maybe his stumps. That his nose, penis, ears and 'all the things that stick out' have fallen off. That later, on discovering his penis has surprisingly not fallen off, he now lacks the arms to wring anything from it. He is also increasingly menaced by an equally unnamed 'they' who may be out to get him, or might just have expectations of him, either of which he'd really rather do without. Further confusing matters, the entire text is constructed from contrapuntal claims like 'it's life trying to get in, no, trying to get him out' and 'I'm a big talking ball, talking about things that do not exist, or that exist perhaps . . .'

Assertion, followed by denial, sometimes followed by reassertion, forms what central thesis *The Unnamable* recognisably contains. For, while our man may be caused to suffer from 'little attacks of hope from time to time', he is most often preoccupied by questions of whether he does or does not, has or will ever, exist at all. And if he is, or is not, currently in the process of dying or of being born. However, even if either were to be the case – and he's not saying they are – he doubts such ephemeral activities could imply greater existential meaning anyway. Because who am I? No one. What's happening? Nothing. What's the point of all this? There isn't one . . . probably. What he really wants is for it all to stop. The talking. The being. The having to go on. But, whenever it does, it just starts again. This is less a novel about 'Life finds a way!' than 'Unfortunately, life finds a way.'

At first glance *The Unnamable* is Beckett at his most bleak, oblique and anti-participatory. Although there is plenty of the writer's almost Wildean black humour – 'To have lost one's limbs and preserved one's dentition, what a mockery!' – as well as his fondness for scatology – '. . . it's like shit, there we have it at last . . .' – the pervasive tone of impotent despair is unignorable. Technically speaking, the novel even advances itself through a process of collapse. Beginning as a fairly traditional-looking text, with paragraphs and punctuation, it gradually breaks down under the weight of its own uncertainty into gigantic strings of speculative subclauses. Eventually it declines into an almost continuous sentence which reflexively, and repeatedly, denies its meaning before it can even shuffle across the finish line of its own full stop. As he himself says, 'To tell the truth, let us be honest at least, it is some considerable time now since I last knew what I was talking about.' A position which is largely impossible for the reader to dispute. That is until, on closer inspection, covert attempts at connection begin to show themselves.

There is the cyclical return to the potential personae of Mahood – Beckett's original title for the novel – and Worm. But are they him, or aren't they? He says they are and aren't. And even if they are, who are they anyway? Is Mahood, with his relentless going forwards, a foreshortened relic of the nineteenth-century Irish immigrant MacHood? Unanswered. And Worm? That squirming, famously eyeless invertebrate, why does he find himself here transformed into a huge lidless eye? A symbol of abjection? Or perversity? A revelation as to the deferent nature of our man? Unconfirmed. There is the repeated suggestion that he may simply be a reincarnation, compound or mere fragment of characters from Beckett's previous novels. Malone is cited, Molloy, Murphy, even Watt. Frequent references to history and mythology also give lie to his argument for the non-existence of a world outside his own. The eternal torment of Prometheus's punishment serves as model for his own compulsive journey through endless speech while William the Silent's motto 'Je maintiendrai/I maintain' is invoked and everyone from St John of the Cross to Toussaint Louverture are put to work. So, for all the insistence on his state of gratuitous isolation, that isolation becomes increasingly populous. It's tempting to suggest that Beckett himself couldn't quite bear to leave the novel out in the cold it claims to exist in. Rather, his 'revelation's' internal logic required an externalisation of the connection between his works. Therefore the inexpugnable unhero of *The Unnamable* cannot escape his genetic debt to his predecessors any more than he will, one day, resist providing parentage for the characters of *Play* and *Endgame*. In this way, all the wilfully vivisected parts – trunk in a jar, severed limbs and disembodied eyes – are ultimately returned to a body once more, wherein they will be made whole again, whether they wish to be or not . . .

If this makes the novel sound like a voyeuristic spectacle of existential suffering though, fear not: the reader suffers too. In classic modernist fashion both voice and reader are abandoned to their respective experiences with little authorial concern for their ensuing discomfort. Certainly, the reader's omnipresent fear that they too are clawing their way through the text towards nothing, never entirely dissipates. However, a clammy awareness does slowly dawn that a point is being made about how inadequate the clubbable comforts of identity are for understanding the deepest nature of self

– the self we truly are beneath the dress-up and linguistic razzamatazz of individualism. *The Unnamable* asks us to be without ourselves, to allow ourselves to be less. To ask of this deflated self, ungarnished by social selfhood, what is left? And what will always remain? Or, when faced with our essential nothingness and the inevitability of suffering, who will we be then? What will we do? '. . . you must go on, I can't go on, I'll go on' the voice says, re-embarking on his purgatorial continuance, while leaving us behind to mull our own.

THE UNNAMABLE

W here now? Who now? When now? Unquestion-
ing. I, say I. Unbelieving. Questions, hypotheses,
call them that. Keep going, going on, call that
going, call that on. Can it be that one day, off it goes
on, that one day I simply stayed in, in where, instead
of going out, in the old way, out to spend day and
night as far away as possible, it wasn't far. Perhaps that
is how it began. You think you are simply resting, the
better to act when the time comes, or for no reason,
and you soon find yourself powerless ever to do anything again. No matter how it happened. It, say it, not
knowing what. Perhaps I simply assented at last to an
old thing. But I did nothing. I seem to speak, it is not
I, about me, it is not about me. These few general
remarks to begin with. What am I to do, what shall I
do, what should I do, in my situation, how proceed?
By aporia pure and simple? Or by affirmations and
negations invalidated as uttered, or sooner or later?
Generally speaking. There must be other shifts.
Otherwise it would be quite hopeless. But it is quite
hopeless. I should mention before going any further,
any further on, that I say aporia without knowing what
it means. Can one be ephectic otherwise than
unawares? I don't know. With the yesses and noes it is
different, they will come back to me as I go along and
how, like a bird, to shit on them all without exception.
The fact would seem to be, if in my situation one may

speak of facts, not only that I shall have to speak of things of which I cannot speak, but also, which is even more interesting, but also that I, which is if possible even more interesting, that I shall have to, I forget, no matter. And at the same time I am obliged to speak. I shall never be silent. Never.

I shall not be alone, in the beginning. I am of course alone. Alone. That is soon said. Things have to be soon said. And how can one be sure, in such darkness? I shall have company. In the beginning. A few puppets. Then I'll scatter them, to the winds, if I can. And things, what is the correct attitude to adopt towards things? And, to begin with, are they necessary? What a question. But I have few illusions, things are to be expected. The best is not to decide anything, in this connection, in advance. If a thing turns up, for some reason or another, take it into consideration. Where there are people, it is said, there are things. Does this mean that when you admit the former you must also admit the latter? Time will tell. The thing to avoid, I don't know why, is the spirit of system. People with things, people without things, things without people, what does it matter, I flatter myself it will not take me long to scatter them, whenever I choose, to the winds. I don't see how. The best would be not to begin. But I have to begin. That is to say I have to go on. Perhaps in the end I shall smother in a throng. Incessant

4

comings and goings, the crush and bustle of a bargain sale. No, no danger. Of that.

Malone is there. Of his mortal liveliness little trace remains. He passes before me at doubtless regular intervals, unless it is I who pass before him. No, once and for all, I do not move. He passes, motionless. But there will not be much on the subject of Malone, from whom there is nothing further to be hoped. Personally I do not intend to be bored. It was while watching him pass that I wondered if we cast a shadow. Impossible to say. He passes close by me, a few feet away, slowly, always in the same direction. I am almost sure it is he. The brimless hat seems to me conclusive. With his two hands he props up his jaw. He passes without a word. Perhaps he does not see me. One of these days I'll challenge him. I'll say, I don't know, I'll say something, I'll think of something when the time comes. There are no days here, but I use the expression. I see him from the waist up, he stops at the waist, as far as I am concerned. The trunk is erect. But I do not know whether he is on his feet or on his knees. He might also be seated. I see him in profile. Sometimes I wonder if it is not Molloy. Perhaps it is Molloy, wearing Malone's hat. But it is more reasonable to suppose it is Malone, wearing his own hat. Oh look, there is the first thing, Malone's hat. I see no other clothes. Perhaps Molloy is not here at all. Could he be, without my knowledge?

The place is no doubt vast. Dim intermittent lights suggest a kind of distance. To tell the truth I believe they are all here, at least from Murphy on, I believe we are all here, but so far I have only seen Malone. Another hypothesis, they were here, but are here no longer. I shall examine it after my fashion. Are there other pits, deeper down? To which one accedes by mine? Stupid obsession with depth. Are there other places set aside for us and this one where I am, with Malone, merely their narthex? I thought I had done with preliminaries. No, no, we have all been here forever, we shall all be here forever, I know it.

No more questions. Is not this rather the place where one finishes vanishing? Will the day come when Malone will pass before me no more? Will the day come when Malone will pass before the spot where I was? Will the day come when another will pass before me, before the spot where I was? I have no opinion, on these matters.

Were I not devoid of feeling his beard would fill me with pity. It hangs down, on either side of his chin, in two twists of unequal length. Was there a time when I too revolved thus? No, I have always been sitting here, at this selfsame spot, my hands on my knees, gazing before me like a great horn-owl in an aviary. The tears stream down my cheeks from my unblink- ing eyes. What makes me weep so? From time to time. There is nothing saddening here. Perhaps it is liquefied brain. Past happiness in any case has clean gone from my memory, assuming it was ever there. If I accomplish other natural functions it is unawares. Nothing ever troubles me. And yet I am troubled. Nothing has ever changed since I have been here. But I dare not infer from this that nothing ever will change. Let us try and see where these considerations lead. I have been here, ever since I began to be, my appearances elsewhere having been put in by other parties. All has proceeded, all this time, in the utmost calm, the most perfect order, apart from one or two manifestations the meaning of which escapes me. No, it is not that their meaning escapes me, my own escapes me just as much. Here all things, no, I shall not say it, being unable to. I owe my existence to no one, these faint fires are not of those that illuminate or burn. Going nowhere, coming from nowhere, Malone passes. These notions of forbears, of houses where lamps are lit at night, and other such, where do they come to me from? And all these questions I ask myself. It is not in a spirit of curiosity. I cannot be silent. About myself I need know nothing. Here all is clear. No, all is not clear. But the discourse must go on. So one invents obscurities. Rhetoric. These lights for instance, which I do not require to mean anything, what is there so strange about them, so wrong? Is it their irregularity, their instability, their shining strong one minute and weak the next, but never beyond the power of one or two candles? Malone appears and disappears with the punctuality of clockwork, always at the same remove, the same velocity, in the same direction, the same attitude. But the play of the lights is truly unpredictable. It is only fair to say that to eyes less knowing than mine they would probably pass unseen. But even to mine do they not sometimes do so? They are perhaps unwavering and fixed and my fitful perceiving the cause of their inconstancy. I hope I may have occasion to revert to this question. But I shall remark without further delay, in order to be sure of doing so, that I am relying on these lights, as indeed on all other similar sources of credible perplexity, to help me continue and perhaps even conclude. I resume, having no alternative. Where was I? Ah yes, from the unexceptionable order which has prevailed here up to date may I infer that such will always be the case? I may of course. But the mere fact of asking myself such a question gives me to reflect. It is in vain I tell myself that its only purpose is to stimulate the lagging discourse, this excellent explanation does not satisfy me. Can it be I am the prey of a genuine pre-occupation, of a need to know as one might say? I don't know. I'll try it another way. If one day a change were to take place, resulting from a principle of disorder already present, or on its way, what then? That would seem to depend on the nature of the change. No, here all change would be fatal and land me back, there and then, in all the fun of the fair. I'll try it another way. Has nothing really changed since I have been here? No, frankly, hand on heart, wait a second, no, nothing, to my knowledge. But, as I have said, the place may well be vast, as it may well measure twelve feet in diameter. It comes to the same thing, as far as discerning its limits is concerned. I like to think I occupy the centre, but nothing is less certain. In a sense I would be better off at the circumference, since my eyes are always fixed in the same direction. But I am certainly not at the circumference. For if I were it would follow that Malone, wheeling about me as he does, would issue from the enceinte at every revolution, which is manifestly impossible. But does he in fact wheel, does he not perhaps simply pass before me in a straight line? No, he wheels, I feel it, and about me, like a planet about its sun. And if he made a noise, as he goes, I would hear him all the time, on my right hand, behind my back, on my left hand, before seeing him again. But he makes none, for I am not deaf, of that I am convinced, that is to say half-convinced. From centre to circumference in any case it is a far cry and I may well be situated some-where between the two. It is equally possible, I do not

9

deny it, that I too am in perpetual motion, accompanied by Malone, as the earth by its moon. In which case there would be no further grounds for my complaining about the disorder of the lights, this being due simply to my insistence on regarding them as always the same lights and viewed always from the same point. All is possible, or almost. But the best is to think of myself as fixed and at the centre of this place, whatever its shape and extent may be. This is also probably the most pleasing to me. In a word, no change apparently since I have been here, disorder of the lights perhaps an illusion, all change to be feared, incomprehensible uneasiness.

That I am not stone deaf is shown by the sounds that reach me. For though the silence here is almost unbroken, it is not completely so. I remember the first sound heard in this place, I have often heard it since. For I am obliged to assign a beginning to my residence here, if only for the sake of clarity. Hell itself, although eternal, dates from the revolt of Lucifer. It is therefore permissible, in the light of this distant analogy, to think of myself as being here forever, but not as having been here forever. This will greatly help me in my relation. Memory notably, which I did not think myself entitled to draw upon, will have its word to say, if necessary. This represents at least a thousand words I was not counting on. I may well be glad of them. So after a long period of immaculate silence a feeble cry was heard, by me. I do not know if Malone heard it too. I was surprised, the word is not too strong. After so long a silence a little cry, stifled outright. What kind of creature uttered it and, if it is the same, still does, from time to time? Impossible to say. Not a human one in any case, there are no human creatures here, or if there are they have done with crying. Is Malone the culprit? Am I? Is it not perhaps a simple little fart, they can be rending? Deplorable mania, when something happens, to inquire what. If only I were not obliged to manifest. And why speak of a cry? Perhaps it is something breaking, some two things colliding. There are sounds here, from time to time, let that suffice. This cry to begin with, since it was the first. And others, rather different. I am getting to know them. I do not know them all. A man may die at the age of seventy without ever having had the possibility of seeing Halley's comet.

It would help me, since to me too I must attribute a beginning, if I could relate it to that of my abode. Did I wait somewhere for this place to be ready to receive me? Or did it wait for me to come and people it? By far the better of these hypotheses, from the point of view of usefulness, is the former, and I shall often have occasion to fall back on it. But both are distasteful. I shall say therefore that our beginnings coincide, that this place was made for me, and I for it, at the same instant.

And the sounds I do not yet know have not yet made themselves heard. But they will change nothing. The cry changed nothing, even the first time. And my surprise? I must have been expecting it.

It is no doubt time I gave a companion to Malone. But first I shall tell of an incident that has only occurred once, so far. I await its recurrence without impatience. Two shapes then, oblong like man, entered into collision before me. They fell and I saw them no more. I naturally thought of the pseudocouple Mercier-Camier. The next time they enter the field, moving slowly towards each other, I shall know they are going to collide, fall and disappear, and this will perhaps enable me to observe them better. Wrong. I continue to see Malone as darkly as the first time. My eyes being fixed always in the same direction I can only see, I shall not say clearly, but as clearly as the visibility permits, that which takes place immediately in front of me, that is to say, in the case before us, the collision, followed by the fall and disappearance. Of their approach I shall never obtain other than a confused glimpse, out of the corner of the eye, and what an eye. For their path too must be a curve, two curves, and meeting I need not say close beside me. For the visibility, unless it be the state of my eyesight, only permits me to see what is close beside me. I may add that my seat would appear to be somewhat elevated, in relation to the surrounding ground, if ground is what it is. Perhaps it is water or some other liquid. With the result that, in order to obtain the optimum view of what takes place in front of me, I should have to lower my eyes a little. But I lower my eyes no more. In a word, I only see what appears immediately in front of me, I only see what appears close beside me, what I best see I see ill.

Why did I have myself represented in the midst of men, the light of day? It seems to me it was none of my doing. We won't go into that now. I can see them still, my delegates. The things they have told me! About men, the light of day. I refused to believe them. But some of it has stuck. But when, through what channels, did I communicate with these gentlemen? Did they intrude on me here? No, no one has ever intruded on me here. Elsewhere then. But I have never been elsewhere. But it can only have been from them I learnt what I know about men and the ways they have of putting up with it. It does not amount to much. I could have dispensed with it. I don't say it was all to no purpose. I'll make use of it, if I'm driven to it. It won't be the first time. What puzzles me is the thought of being indebted for this information to persons with whom I can never have been in contact. Can it be innate knowledge? Like that of good and evil. This seems improbable to me. Innate knowledge of my mother, for example, is that conceivable? Not for me.

She was one of their favourite subjects, of conversation. They also gave me the low-down on God. They told me I depended on him, in the last analysis. They had it on the reliable authority of his agents at Bally I forget what, this being the place, according to them, where the inestimable gift of life had been rammed down my gullet. But what they were most determined for me to swallow was my fellow-creatures. In this they were without mercy. I remember little or nothing of these lectures. I cannot have understood a great deal. But I seem to have retained certain descriptions, in spite of myself. They gave me courses on love, on intelligence, most precious, most precious. They also taught me to count, and even to reason. Some of this rubbish has come in handy on occasions, I don't deny it, on occasions which would never have arisen if they had left me in peace. I use it still, to scratch my arse with. Low types they must have been, their pockets full of poison and antidote. Perhaps all this instruction was by correspondence. And yet I seem to know their faces. From photographs perhaps. When did all this nonsense stop? And has it stopped? A few last questions. Is it merely a lull? There were four or five of them at me, they called that presenting their report. One in particular, Basil I think he was called, filled me with hatred. Without opening his mouth, fastening on me his eyes like cinders with all their seeing, he changed me a little more each time into what he wanted me to be. Is he still glaring at me, from the shadows? Is he still usurping my name, the one they foisted on me, up there in their world, patiently, from season to season? No no, here I am in safety, amusing myself wondering who can have dealt me these insignificant wounds.

The other advances full upon me. He emerges as from heavy hangings, advances a few steps, looks at me, then backs away. He is stooping and seems to be dragging invisible burdens. What I see best is his hat. The crown is all worn through, like the sole of an old boot, giving vent to a straggle of grey hairs. He raises his eyes and I feel the long imploring gaze, as if I could do something for him. Another impression, no doubt equally false, he brings me presents and dare not give them. He takes them away again, or he lets them fall, and they vanish. He does not come often, I cannot be more precise, but regularly assuredly. His visit has never coincided, up to now, with the transit of Malone. But perhaps some day it will. That would not necessarily be a violation of the order prevailing here. For if I can work out to within a few inches the orbit of Malone, assuming perhaps erroneously that he passes before me at a distance of say three feet, with regard to the other's career I must remain in the dark. For I am incapable not only of measuring time, which in itself is sufficient to vitiate all calculation in this connection, but also of comparing their respective velocities. So I cannot tell if I shall ever have the good fortune to see the two of them at once. But I am inclined to think I shall. For if I were never to see the two of them at once, then it would follow, or should follow, that between their respective appearances the interval never varies. No, wrong. For the interval may vary considerably, and indeed it seems to me it does, without ever being abolished. Nevertheless I am inclined to think, because of this erratic interval, that my two visitors may some day meet before my eyes, collide and perhaps even knock each other down. I have said that all things here recur sooner or later, no, I was going to say it, then thought better of it. But is it not possible that this does not apply to encounters? The only encounter I ever witnessed, a long time ago now, has never yet been re-enacted. It was perhaps the end of something. And I shall perhaps be delivered of Malone and the other, not that they disturb me, the day I see the two of them at one and the same time, that is to say in collision. Unfortunately they are not the only disturbers of my peace. Others come towards me, pass before me, wheel about me. And no doubt others still, invisible so far. I repeat they do not disturb me. But in the long run it might become wearisome. I don't see how. But the possibility must be taken into account. One starts things moving without a thought of how to stop them.

In order to speak. One starts speaking as if it were possible to stop at will. It is better so. The search for the means to put an end to things, an end to speech, is what enables the discourse to continue. No, I must not try to think, simply utter. Method or no method I shall have to banish them in the end, the beings, things, shapes, sounds and lights with which my haste to speak has encumbered this place. In the frenzy of utterance the concern with truth. Hence the interest of a possible deliverance by means of encounter. But not so fast. First dirty, then make clean.

Perhaps it is time I paid a little attention to myself, for a change. I shall be reduced to it sooner or later. At first sight it seems impossible. Me, utter me, in the same foul breath as my creatures? Say of me that I see this, feel that, fear, hope, know and do not know? Yes, I will say it, and of me alone. Impassive, still and mute, Malone revolves, a stranger forever to my infirmities, one who is not as I can never not be. I am motionless in vain, he is the god. And the other? I have assigned him eyes that implore me, offerings for me, need of succour. He does not look at me, does not know of me, wants for nothing. I alone am man and all the rest divine.

Air, the air, is there anything to be squeezed from that old chestnut? Close to me it is grey, dimly transparent, and beyond that charmed circle deepens and spreads its fine impenetrable veils. Is it I who cast the faint light that enables me to see what goes on under my nose? There is nothing to be gained, for the moment, by supposing so. There is no night so deep, so I have heard tell, that it may not be pierced in the end, with the help of no other light than that of the blackened sky, or of the earth itself. Nothing nocturnal here. This grey, first murky, then frankly opaque, is luminous none the less. But may not this screen which my eyes probe in vain, and see as denser air, in reality be the enclosure wall, as compact as lead? To elucidate this point I would need a stick or pole, and the means of plying it, the former being of little avail without the latter, and vice versa. I could also do, incidentally, with future and conditional participles. Then I would dart it, like a javelin, straight before me and know, by the sound made, whether that which hems me round, and blots out my world, is the old void, or a plenum. Or else, without letting it go, I would wield it like a sword and thrust it through empty air, or against the barrier. But the days of sticks are over, here I can count on my body alone, my body incapable of the smallest movement and whose very eyes can no longer close as they once could, according to Basil and his crew, to rest me from seeing, to rest me from waking, to darken me to sleep, and no longer look away, or down, or up open to heaven, but must remain forever fixed and staring on the narrow space before them where there is nothing to be seen, 99 per cent of the time. They must be as red as live coals. I sometimes wonder if the two retinae are not facing each other. And come to think of it this grey is shot with rose, like the plumage of certain birds, among which I seem to remember the cockatoo.

Whether all grow black, or all grow bright, or all remain grey, it is grey we need, to begin with, because of what it is, and of what it can do, made of bright and black, able to shed the former, or the latter, and be the latter or the former alone. But perhaps I am the prey, on the subject of grey, in the grey, to delusions.

How, in such conditions, can I write, to consider only the manual aspect of that bitter folly? I don't know. I could know. But I shall not know. Not this time. It is I who write, who cannot raise my hand from my knee. It is I who think, just enough to write, whose head is far. I am Matthew and I am the angel, I who came before the cross, before the sinning, came into the world, came here.

I add this, to be on the safe side. These things I say, and shall say, if I can, are no longer, or are not yet, or never were, or never will be, or if they were, if they are, if they will be, were not here, are not here, will not be here, but elsewhere. But I am here. So I am obliged to add this. I who am here, who cannot speak, cannot think, and who must speak, and therefore perhaps think a little, cannot in relation only to me who am here, to here where I am, but can a little, sufficiently, I don't know how, unimportant, in relation to me who was elsewhere, who shall be elsewhere, and to those places where I was, where I shall be. But I have never been elsewhere, however uncertain the future. And the simplest therefore is to say that what I say, what I shall say, if I can, relates to the place where I am, to me who am there, in spite of my inability to think of these, or to speak of them, because of the compulsion I am under to speak of them, and therefore perhaps think of them a little. Another thing. What I say, what I may say, on this subject, the subject of me and my abode, has already been said since, having always been here, I am here still. At last a piece of reasoning that pleases me, and worthy of my situation. So I have no cause for anxiety. And yet I am anxious. So I am not heading for disaster, I am not heading anywhere, my adventures are over, my say said, I call that my adventures. And yet I feel not. And indeed I greatly fear, since my speech can only be of me and here, that I am once more engaged in putting an end to both. Which would not matter, far from it, but for the obligation, once rid of them, to begin again, to start again from nowhere, from no one and from nothing and win to me again, to me here again, by fresh ways to be sure, or by the ancient ways, unrecognisable at each fresh faring. Whence a certain confusion in the exordia, long enough to situate the condemned and prepare him for execution. And yet I do not despair of one day sparing me, without going silent. And that day, I don't know why, I shall be able to go silent, and make an end, I know it. Yes, the hope is there, once again, of not making me, not losing me, of staying here, where I said I have always been, but I had to say something quick, of ending here, it would be wonderful. But is it to be wished? Yes, it is to be wished, to end would be wonderful, no matter who I am, no matter where I am.

I hope this preamble will soon come to an end and the statement begin that will dispose of me. Unfortunately I am afraid, as always, of going on. For to go on means going from here, means finding me, losing me, vanishing and beginning again, a stranger first, then little by little the same as always, in another place, where I shall say I have always been, of which I shall know nothing, being incapable of seeing, moving, thinking, speaking, but of which little by little, in spite of these handicaps, I shall begin to know something, just enough for it to turn out to be the same place as always, the same which seems made for me and does not want me, which I seem to want and do not want, take your choice, which spews me out or swallows me up, I'll never know, which is perhaps merely the inside of my distant skull where once I wandered, now am fixed, lost for tininess, or straining against the walls, with my head, my hands, my feet, my back, and ever murmuring my old stories, my old story, as if it were the first time. So there is nothing to be afraid of. And yet I am afraid, afraid of what my words will do to me, to my refuge, yet again. Is there really nothing new to try? I mentioned my hope, but it is not serious. If I could speak and yet say nothing, really nothing? Then I might escape being gnawed to death as by an old satiated rat, and my little tester-bed along with me, a cradle, or be gnawed to death not so fast, in my old cradle, and the torn flesh have time to knit, as in the Caucasus, before being torn again. But it seems impossible to speak and yet say nothing, you think you have succeeded, but you always overlook something, a little yes, a little no, enough to exterminate a regiment of dragoons. And yet I do not despair, this time, while saying who I am, where I am, of not losing me, of not going from here, of ending here. What prevents the miracle is the spirit of method to which I have perhaps been a little too addicted. The fact that Prometheus was delivered twenty-nine thousand nine hundred and seventy years after having purged his offence leaves me naturally as cold as camphor. For between me and that miscreant who mocked the gods, invented fire, denatured clay and domesticated the horse, in a word obliged humanity, I trust there is nothing in common. But the thing is worth mentioning. In a word, shall I be able to speak of me and of this place without putting an end to us, shall I ever be able to go silent, is there any connection between these two questions? Nothing like issues. There are a few to be going on with, perhaps one only.

All these Murphys, Molloys and Malones do not fool me. They have made me waste my time, suffer for nothing, speak of them when, in order to stop speaking, I should have spoken of me and of me alone. But I just said I have spoken of me, am speaking of me. I don't care a curse what I just said. It is now I shall speak of me, for the first time. I thought I was right in enlisting these sufferers of my pains. I was wrong. They never suffered my pains, their pains are nothing, compared to mine, a mere tittle of mine, the tittle I thought I could put from me, in order to witness it. Let them be gone now, them and all the others, those I have used and those I have not used, give me back the pains I lent them and vanish, from my life, my memory, my terrors and shames. There, now there is no one here but me, no one wheels about me, no one comes towards me, no one has ever met anyone before my eyes, these creatures have never been, only I and this black void have ever been. And the sounds? No, all is silent. And the lights, on which I had set such store, must they too go out? Yes, out with them, there is no light here. No grey either, black is what I should have said. Nothing then but me, of which I know nothing, except that I have never uttered, and this black, of which I know nothing either, except that it is black, and empty. That then is what, since I have to speak, I shall speak of, until I need speak no more. And Basil and his gang? Inexistent, invented to explain I forget what. Ah yes, all lies, God and man, nature and the light of day, the heart's outpourings and the means of understanding, all invented, basely, by me alone, with the help of no one, since there is no one, to put off the hour when I must speak of me. There will be no more about them.

I, of whom I know nothing, I know my eyes are open, because of the tears that pour from them unceasingly. I know I am seated, my hands on my knees, because of the pressure against my rump, against the soles of my feet, against the palms of my hands, against my knees. Against my palms the pressure is of my knees, against my knees of my palms, but what is it that presses against my rump, against the soles of my feet? I don't know. My spine is not supported. I mention these details to make sure I am not lying on my back, my legs raised and bent, my eyes closed. It is well to establish the position of the body from the outset, before passing on to more important matters. But what makes me say I gaze straight before me, as I have said? I feel my back straight, my neck stiff and free of twist and up on top of it the head, like the ball of the cup-and-ball in its cup at the end of the stick. These comparisons are uncalled for. Then there is the way of flowing of my tears which flow all over my face, and even down along the neck, in a way it seems to me they could not do if the face were bowed, or lifted up. But I must not confuse the unbowed head with the level gaze, nor the vertical with the horizontal plane. This question in any case is secondary, since I see nothing. Am I clothed? I have often asked myself this question, then suddenly started talking about Malone's hat, or Molloy's greatcoat, or Murphy's suit. If I am, I am but lightly. For I feel my tears coursing over my chest, my sides, and all down my back. Ah yes, I am truly bathed in tears. They gather in my beard and from there, when it can hold no more – no, no beard, no hair either, it is a great smooth ball I carry on my shoulders, featureless, but for the eyes, of which only the sockets remain. And were it not for the distant testimony of my palms, my soles, which I have not yet been able to quash, I would gladly give myself the shape, if not the consistency, of an egg, with two holes no matter where to prevent it from bursting, for the consistency is more like that of mucilage. But softly, softly, otherwise I'll never arrive. In the matter of clothes then I can think of nothing for the moment but possibly puttees, with perhaps a few rags clinging to me here and there. No more obscenities either. Why should I have a sex, who have no longer a nose? All those things have fallen, all the things that stick out, with my eyes, my hair, without leaving a trace, fallen so far, so deep, that I heard nothing, perhaps are falling still, my hair slowly like soot still, of the fall of my ears heard nothing. Mean words, and needless, from the mean old spirit, I invented love, music, the smell of flowering currant, to escape from me. Organs, a without, it's easy to imagine, a god, it's unavoidable, you imagine them, it's easy, the worst is dulled, you doze away, an instant. Yes, God, fomenter of calm, I never believed, not a second. No more pauses either. Can I keep nothing then, nothing of what has borne my poor thoughts, bent beneath my words, while I hid? I'll dry these streaming sockets too, bung them up, there, it's done, no more tears, I'm a big talking ball, talking about things that do not exist, or that exist perhaps, impossible to know, beside the point. Ah yes, quick let me change my tune. And after all why a ball, rather than something else, and why big? Why not a cylinder, a small cylinder? An egg, a medium egg? No no, that's the old nonsense, I always knew I was round, solid and round, without daring to say so, no asperities, no apertures, invisible perhaps, or as vast as Sirius in the Great Dog, these expressions mean nothing. All that matters is that I am round and hard, there must be reasons for that, for my being round and hard rather than of some irregular shape and subject to the dents and bulges incident to shock, but I have done with reasons. All the rest I renounce, including this ridiculous black which I thought for a moment worthier than grey to enfold me. What rubbish all this stuff about light and dark. And how I have luxuriated in it. But do I roll, in the manner of a true ball? Or am I in equilibrium somewhere, on one of my numberless poles? I feel strongly tempted to inquire. What reams of discourse I could elicit from this seemingly so legitimate preoccupation. But which would not be credited to me. No, between me and the right to silence, the living rest, stretches the same old lesson, the one I once knew by heart and would not say, I don't know why, perhaps for fear of silence, or thinking any old thing would do, and so for preference lies, in order to remain hidden, no importance. But now I shall say my old lesson, if I can remember it. Under the skies, on the roads, in the towns, in the woods, in the hills, in the plains, by the shores, on the seas, behind my manni-kins, I was not always sad, I wasted my time, abjured my rights, suffered for nothing, forgot my lesson. Then a little hell after my own heart, not too cruel, with a few nice damned to foist my groans on, something sighing off and on and the distant gleams of pity's fires biding their hour to promote us to ashes. I speak, speak, because I must, but I do not listen, I seek my lesson, my life I used to know and would not confess, hence

27

possibly an occasional slight lack of limpidity. And perhaps now again I shall do no more than seek my lesson, to the self-accompaniment of a tongue that is not mine. But instead of saying what I should not have said, and what I shall say no more, if I can, and what I shall say perhaps, if I can, should I not rather say some other thing, even though it be not yet the right thing? I'll try, I'll try in another present, even though it be not yet mine, without pauses, without tears, without eyes, without reasons. Let it be assumed then that I am at rest, though this is unimportant, at rest or forever moving, through the air or in contact with other surfaces, or that I sometimes move, sometimes rest, since I feel nothing, neither quietude nor change, nothing that can serve as a point of departure towards an opinion on this subject, which would not greatly matter if I possessed some general notions, and then the use of reason, but there it is, I feel nothing, know nothing, and as far as thinking is concerned I do just enough to preserve me from going silent, you can't call that thinking. Let us then assume nothing, neither that I move, nor that I don't, it's safer, since the thing is unimportant, and pass on to those that are. Namely? This voice that speaks, knowing that it lies, indifferent to what it says, too old perhaps and too abased ever to succeed in saying the words that would be its last, knowing itself useless and its uselessness in vain, not listening to itself but to the silence that it breaks and whence perhaps one day will come stealing the long clear sigh of advent and farewell, is it one? I'll ask no more questions, there are no more questions, I know none any more. It issues from me, it fills me, it clamours against my walls, it is not mine, I can't stop it, I can't prevent it, from tearing me, racking me, assailing me. It is not mine, I have none, I have no voice and must speak, that is all I know, it's round that I must revolve, of that I must speak, with this voice that is not mine, but can only be mine, since there is no one but me, or if there are others, to whom it might belong, they have never come near me. I won't delay just now to make this clear. Perhaps they are watching me from afar, I have no objection, as long as I don't see them, watching me like a face in the embers which they know is doomed to crumble, but it takes too long, it's getting late, eyes are heavy and tomorrow they must rise betimes. So it is I who speak, all alone, since I can't do otherwise. No, I am speechless. Talking of speaking, what if I went silent? What would happen to me then? Worse than what is happening? But fie these are questions again. That is typical. I know no more questions and they keep on pouring out of my mouth. I think I know what it is, it's to prevent the discourse from coming to an end, this futile discourse which is not credited to me and brings me not a syllable nearer silence. But now I am on my guard, I shall not answer them any more, I shall not pretend any more to answer them. Perhaps I shall be obliged, in order not to peter out, to invent another fairy-tale, yet another, with heads, trunks, arms, legs and all that follows, let loose in the changeless round of imperfect shadow and dubious light. But I hope and trust not. But I always can if necessary. For while unfolding my facetiae, the last time that happened to me, or to the other who passes for me, I was not inattentive. And it seemed to me then that I heard a murmur telling of another and less unpleasant method of ending my troubles and that I even succeeded in catching, without ceasing for an instant to emit my he said, and he said to himself, and he asked, and he answered, a certain number of highly promising formulae and which indeed I promised myself to turn to good account at the first opportunity, that is to say as soon as I had finished with my troop of lunatics. But all has gone clean from my head. For it is difficult to speak, even any old rubbish, and at the same time focus one's attention on another point, where one's true interest lies, as fitfully defined by a feeble murmur seeming to apologise for not being dead. And what it seemed to me I heard then, concerning what I should do, and say, in order to have nothing further to do, nothing further to say, it seemed to me I only barely heard it, because of the noise I was engaged in making elsewhere, in

obedience to the unintelligible terms of an incomprehensible damnation. And yet I was sufficiently
impressed by certain expressions to make a vow, while
continuing my yelps, never to forget them and, what is
more, to ensure they should engender others and
finally, in an irresistible torrent, banish from my vile
mouth all other utterance, from my mouth spent in
vain with vain inventions all other utterance but theirs,
the true at last, the last at last. But all is forgotten and I
have done nothing, unless what I am doing now is
something, and nothing could give me greater satisfaction. For if I could hear such a music at such a time, I
mean while floundering through a ponderous chronicle
of moribunds in their courses, moving, clashing, writhing or fallen in short-lived swoons, with how much
more reason should I not hear it now, when supposedly
I am burdened with myself alone. But this is thinking
again. And I see myself slipping, though not yet at the
last extremity, towards the resorts of fable. Would it not
be better if I were simply to keep on saying babababa,
for example, while waiting to ascertain the true function of this venerable organ? Enough questions, enough
reasoning, I resume, years later, meaning I suppose
that I went silent, that I can go silent. And now this
noise again. That is all rather obscure. I say years,
though here there are no years. What matter how long?
Years is one of Basil's ideas. A short time, a long time,

it's all the same. I kept silence, that's all that counts, if that counts, I have forgotten if that is supposed to count. And now it is taken from me again. Silence, yes, but what silence! For it is all very fine to keep silence, but one has also to consider the kind of silence one keeps. I listened. One might as well speak and be done with it. What liberty! I strained my ear towards what must have been my voice still, so weak, so far, that it was like the sea, a far calm sea dying – no, none of that, no beach, no shore, the sea is enough, I've had enough of shingle, enough of sand, enough of earth, enough of sea too. Decidedly Basil is becoming import-ant, I'll call him Mahood instead, I prefer that, I'm queer. It was he told me stories about me, lived in my stead, issued forth from me, came back to me, entered back into me, heaped stories on my head. I don't know how it was done. I always liked not knowing, but Mahood said it wasn't right. He didn't know either, but it worried him. It is his voice which has often, always, mingled with mine, and sometimes drowned it com-pletely. Until he left me for good, or refused to leave me any more, I don't know. Yes, I don't know if he's here now or far away, but I don't think I am far wrong in saying that he has ceased to plague me. When he was away I tried to find myself again, to forget what he had said, about me, about my misfortunes, fatuous mis-fortunes, idiotic pains, in the light of my true situation, revolting word. But his voice continued to testify for me, as though woven into mine, preventing me from saying who I was, what I was, so as to have done with saying, done with listening. And still today, as he would say, though he plagues me no more his voice is there, in mine, but less, less. And being no longer renewed it will disappear one day, I hope, from mine, completely. But in order for that to happen I must speak, speak. And at the same time, I do not deceive myself, he may come back again, or go away again and then come back again. Then my voice, the voice, would say, That's an idea, now I'll tell one of Mahood's stories, I need a rest. Yes, that's how it would happen. And it would say, Then refreshed, set about the truth again, with redoubled vigour. To make me think I was a free agent. But it would not be my voice, not even in part. That is how it would be done. Or quietly, stealthily, the story would begin, as if nothing had happened and I still the teller and the told. But I would be fast asleep, my mouth agape, as usual, I would look the same as usual. And from my sleeping mouth the lies would pour, about me. No, not sleeping, listening, in tears. But now, is it I now, I on me? Sometimes I think it is. And then I realise it is not. I am doing my best, and failing again, yet again. I don't mind failing, it's a pleasure, but I want to go silent. Not as just now, the better to listen, but peacefully, victorious, without ulterior object. Then it would be a life worth having, a life at last. My speech-parched voice at rest would fill with spittle, I'd let it flow over and over, happy at last, dribbling with life, my pensum ended, in the silence. I spoke, I must have spoken, of a lesson, it was pensum I should have said, I confused pensum with lesson. Yes, I have a pensum to discharge, before I can be free, free to dribble, free to speak no more, listen no more, and I've forgotten what it is. There at last is a fair picture of my situation. I was given a pensum, at birth perhaps, as a punishment for having been born perhaps, or for no particular reason, because they dislike me, and I've forgotten what it is. But was I ever told? Squeeze, squeeze, not too hard, but squeeze a little longer, this is perhaps about you, and your goal at hand. After ten thousand words? Well let us say one goal, after it there will be others. Speak, yes, but to me, I have never spoken enough to me, never listened enough to me, never replied enough to me, never had pity enough on me, I have spoken for my master, listened for the words of my master never spoken, Well done, my child, well done, my son, you may stop, you may go, you are free, you are acquitted, you are pardoned, never spoken. My master. There is a vein I must not lose sight of. But for the moment my concern – but before I forget, there may be more than one, a whole college of tyrants, differing in their views as to what should be done with me, in conclave since time began or a little later, listening to me from time to time, then breaking up for a meal or a game of cards – my concern is with the pensum of which I think I may safely say, without loss of face, that it is in some way related to that lesson too hastily proclaimed, too hastily denied. For all I need say is this, that if I have a pensum to perform it is because I could not say my lesson, and that when I have finished my pensum I shall still have my lesson to say, before I have the right to stay quiet in my corner, alive and dribbling, my mouth shut, my tongue at rest, far from all disturbance, all sound, my mind at peace, that is to say empty. But this does not get me very far. For even should I hit upon the right pensum, somewhere in this churn of words at last, I would still have to reconstitute the right lesson, unless of course the two are one and the same, which obviously is not impossible either. Strange notion in any case, and eminently open to suspicion, that of a task to be performed, before one can be at rest. Strange task, which consists in speaking of oneself. Strange hope, turned towards silence and peace. Possessed of nothing but my voice, the voice, it may seem natural, once the idea of obligation has been swallowed, that I should interpret it as an obligation to say something. But is it possible? Bereft of hands, perhaps it is my duty to clap or, striking the palms together, to call the waiter, and of feet, to dance the Carmagnole. But let us first suppose, in order to get on a little, then we'll suppose something else, in order to get on a little further, that it is in fact required of me that I say something, something that is not to be found in all I have said up to now. That seems a reasonable assumption. But thence to infer that the something required is something about me suddenly strikes me as unwarranted. Might it not rather be the praise of my master, intoned, in order to obtain his forgiveness? Or the admission that I am Mahood after all and these stories of a being whose identity he usurps, and whose voice he prevents from being heard, all lies from beginning to end? And what if Mahood were my master? I'll leave it at that, for the time being. So many prospects in so short a time, it's too much. Decidedly it seems impossible, at this stage, that I should dispense with questions, as I promised myself I would. No, I merely swore I'd stop asking them. And perhaps before long, who knows, I shall light on the happy combination which will prevent them from ever arising again in my – let us not be over-nice – mind. For what I am doing is not being done without a minimum of mind. Not mine perhaps, granted, with pleasure, but I draw on it, at least I try and look as if I did. Rich matter there, to be exploited, fatten you up, suck it to the core, keep you going for years, tasty into the bargain, I quiver at the thought, give you my word, spoken in jest, quiver and hurry on, all life before me, on and forget, what I was saying, just now, something important, it's gone, it'll come back, no regrets, as good as new, unrecognisable, let's hope so, some day when I feel more on for high-class nuts to crack. On. The master. I never paid him enough attention. No more perhapses either, that old trick is worn to a thread. I'll forbid myself everything, then go on as if I hadn't. The master. A few allusions here and there, as to a satrap, with a view to enlisting sympathy. They clothed me and gave me money, that kind of thing, the light touch. Then no more. Or Moran's boss, I forget his name. Ah yes, certain things, things I invented, hoping for the best, full of doubts, croaking with fatigue, I remember certain things, not always the same. But to investigate this matter seriously, I mean with as much futile ardour as that of the underling, which I hoped was mine, close to mine, the road to mine, no, that never occurred to me. And if it occurs to me now it is because I have despaired of mine. A moment of discouragement, to strike while hot. My master then, assuming he is solitary, in my image, wishes me well, poor devil, wishes my good, and if he does not seem to do very much in order not to be disappointed it is because there is not very much to be done or, better still, because there is nothing to be done, otherwise he would have done it, my great and good master, that must be it, long ago, poor devil. Another supposition, he has taken the

37

necessary steps, his will is done as far as I am concerned (for he may have other protégés) and all is well with me without my knowing it. Cases one and two. I'll consider the former first, if I can. Then I'll admire the latter, if my eyes are still open. This sounds like one of Malone's anecdotes. But quick, consider, before you forget. There he is then, the unfortunate brute, quite miserable because of me, for whom there is nothing to be done, and he so anxious to help, so used to giving orders and to being obeyed. There he is, ever since I came into the world, possibly at his instigation, I wouldn't put it past him, commanding me to be well, you know, in every way, no complaints at all, with as much success as if he were shouting at a lump of inanimate matter. If he is not pleased with this panegyric I hope I may be – I nearly said hanged, but that I hope in any case, without restriction, I nearly said con, that would cut my cackle. Ah for a neck! I want all to be well with you, do you hear me, that's what he keeps on dinning at me. To which I reply, in a respectful attitude, I too, your Lordship. I say that to cheer him up, he sounds so unhappy. I am good-hearted, on the surface. No, we have no conversation, never a mum of his mouth to me. He's out of luck, that's certain, perhaps he didn't choose me. What he means by good, my good, is another problem. He is capable of wanting me to be happy, such a thing has been known, it appears. Or to serve a purpose. Or the two at once! A little more explicitness on his part, since the initiative belongs to him, might be a help, as well from his point of view as from the one he attributes to me. Let the man explain himself and have done with it. It's none of my business to ask him questions, even if I knew how to reach him. Let him inform me once and for all what exactly it is he wants from me, for me. What he wants is my good, I know that, at least I say it, in the hope of bringing him round to a more reasonable frame of mind, assuming he exists and, existing, hears me. But what good, there must be more than one. The supreme perhaps. In a word let him enlighten me, that's all I ask, so that I may at least have the satisfaction of knowing in what sense I leave to be desired. If he wants me to say something, for my good naturally, he has only to tell me what it is and I'll let it out with a roar straight away. It's true he may have already told me a hundred times. Well, let him make it a hundred and one, this time I'll try and pay attention. But perhaps I malign him unjustly, my good master, perhaps he is not solitary like me, not free like me, but associated with others, equally good, equally concerned with my welfare, but differing as to its nature. Every day, up above, I mean up above me, from one set hour to another set hour, everything there being set and settled except what is to be done with me, they assemble to discuss me. Or perhaps it's a meeting of deputies, with instructions to elaborate a tentative agreement. The fact of my continuing, while they are thus engaged, to be what I have always been is naturally preferable to a lame resolution, voted perhaps by a majority of one, or drawn from an old hat. They too are unhappy, all this time, each one to the best of his capacity, because all is not well with me. And now enough of that. If that doesn't mollify them so much the worse for me, I can still conceive of such a thing. But one more suggestion before I forget and go on to serious matters. Why don't they wash their hands of me and set me free? That might do me good. I don't know. Perhaps then I could go silent, for good and all. Idle talk, idle talk, I am free, abandoned. All for nothing again. Even Mahood has left me, I'm alone. All this business of a labour to accomplish, before I can end, of words to say, a truth to recover, in order to say it, before I can end, of an imposed task, once known, long neglected, finally forgotten, to perform, before I can be done with speaking, done with listening, I invented it all, in the hope it would console me, help me to go on, allow me to think of myself as somewhere on a road, moving, between a beginning and an end, gaining ground, losing ground, getting lost, but somehow in the long run making headway. All lies. I have nothing to do, that is to say nothing in particular. I have to speak, whatever that means. Having nothing to say, no words but the words of others, I have to speak. No one compels me to, there is no one, it's an accident, a fact. Nothing can ever exempt me from it, there is nothing, nothing to discover, nothing to recover, nothing that can lessen what remains to say, I have the ocean to drink, so there is an ocean then. Not to have been a dupe, that will have been my best possession, my best deed, to have been a dupe, wishing I wasn't, thinking I wasn't, knowing I was, not being a dupe of not being a dupe. For any old thing, no, that doesn't work, that should work, but it doesn't. Labyrinthine torment that can't be grasped, or limited, or felt, or suffered, no, not even suffered, I suffer all wrong too, even that I do all wrong too, like an old turkey-hen dying on her feet, her back covered with chickens and the rats spying on her. Next instalment, quick. No cries, above all no cries, be urbane, a credit to the art and code of dying, while the others cackle, I can hear them from here, like the crackling of thorns, no, I forgot, it's impossible, it's myself I hear, howling behind my dissertation. So not any old thing. Even Mahood's stories are not any old thing, though no less foreign, to what, to that unfamiliar native land of mine, as unfamiliar as that other where men come and go, and feel at home, on tracks they have made themselves, in order to visit one another with the maximum of convenience and dispatch, in the light of a choice of luminaries pissing on the darkness turn about, so that it is never dark, never deserted, that must be terrible. So be it. Not any old thing, but as near as no matter. Mahood. Before him there were others, taking themselves for me, it must be a sinecure handed down from generation to generation, to judge by their family air. Mahood is no worse than his predecessors. But before executing his portrait, full length on his surviving leg, let me note that my next vice-exister will be a billy in the bowl, that's final, with his bowl on his head and his arse in the dust, plump down on thousand-breasted Tellus, it'll be softer for him. Faith that's an idea, yet another, mutilate, mutilate, and perhaps some day, fifteen generations hence, you'll succeed in beginning to look like yourself, among the passers-by. In the meantime it's Mahood, this caricature is he. What if we were one and the same after all, as he affirms, and I deny? And I been in the places where he says I have been, instead of having stayed on here, trying to take advantage of his absence to unravel my tangle? Here, in my domain, what is Mahood doing in my domain, and how does he get here? There I am launched again on the same old hopeless business, there we are face to face, Mahood and I, if we are twain, as I say we are. I never saw him, I don't see him, he has told me what he is like, what I am like, they have all told me that, it must be one of their principal functions. It isn't enough that I should know what I'm doing, I must also know what I'm looking like. This time I am short of a leg. And yet it appears I have rejuvenated. That's part of the programme. Having brought me to death's door, senile gangrene, they whip off a leg and yip off I go again, like a young one, scouring the earth for a hole to hide in. A single leg and other distinctive stigmata to go with it, human to be sure, but not exaggeratedly, lest I take fright and refuse to nibble. He'll resign himself in the end, he'll own up in the end, that's the watchword. Let's try him this time with a hairless wedge-head, he might fancy that, that kind of talk. With the solitary leg in the middle, that might appeal to him. The poor bastards. They could clap an artificial anus in the hollow of my hand and still I wouldn't be there, alive with their life, not far short of a man, just barely a man, sufficiently a man to have hopes one day of being one, my avatars behind me. And yet sometimes it seems to me I am there, among the incriminated scenes, tottering under the attributes peculiar to the lords of creation, dumb with howling to be put out of my misery, and all round me the spinach blue rustling with satisfaction. Yes, more than once I almost took myself for the other, all but suffered after his fashion, the space of an instant. Then they uncorked the champagne. One of us at last! Green with anguish! A real little terrestrial! Choking in the chlorophyll! Hugging the slaughterhouse walls!

43

Paltry priests of the irrepressible ephemeral, how they must hate me. Come, my lambkin, join in our gambols, it's soon over, you'll see, just time to frolic with a lamb-kinette, that's jam. Love, there's a carrot never fails, I always had to thread some old bodkin. And that's the kind of jakes in which I sometimes dreamt I dwelt, and even let down my trousers. Mahood himself nearly codded me more than once. I've been he an instant, hobbling through a nature which, it is only fair to say, was on the barren side and, what is more, it is only just to add, tolerably deserted to begin with. After each thrust of my crutches I stopped, to devour a narcotic and measure the distance gone, the distance yet to go. My head is there too, broad at the base, its slopes denuded, culminating in a ridge or crowning glory strewn with long waving hairs like those that grow on naevi. No denying it, I'm confoundedly well informed. You must allow it was tempting. I say an instant, perhaps it was years. Then I withdrew my adhesion, it was getting too much of a good thing. I had already advanced a good ten paces, if one may call them paces, not in a straight line I need hardly say, but in a sharp curve which, if I continued to follow it, seemed likely to restore me to my point of departure, or to one adja-cent. I must have got embroiled in a kind of inverted spiral, I mean one the coils of which, instead of widen-ing more and more, grew narrower and narrower and finally, given the kind of space in which I was supposed to evolve, would come to an end for lack of room. Faced then with the material impossibility of going any further I should no doubt have had to stop, unless of course I elected to set off again at once in the opposite direction, to unscrew myself as it were, after having screwed myself to a standstill, which would have been an experience rich in interest and fertile in surprises if I am to believe what I once was told, in spite of my protests, namely that there is no road so dull, on the way out, but it has quite a different aspect, quite a different dullness, on the way back, and vice versa. No good wriggling, I'm a mine of useless knowledge. But a difficulty arises here. For if by dint of winding myself up, if I may venture that ellipse, it doesn't often happen to me now, if by dint of winding myself up, I don't seem to have gained much time, if by dint of winding myself up I must inevitably find myself stuck in the end, once launched in the opposite direction should I not normally unfold ad infinitum, with no possibility of ever stopping, the space in which I was marooned being globular, or is it the earth, no matter, I know what I mean. But where is the difficulty? There was one a moment ago, I could swear to it. Not to mention that I could quite easily at any moment, literally any, run foul of a wall, a tree or similar obstacle, which of course it would be prohibited to circumvent, and thereby have

45

an end put to my gyrations as effectively as by the kind of cramp just mentioned. But obstacles, it appears, can be removed in the fullness of time, but not by me, me they would stop dead forever, if I lived among them. But even without such aids it seems to me that once beyond the equator you would start turning inwards again, out of sheer necessity, I somehow have that feeling. At the particular moment I am referring to, I mean when I took myself for Mahood, I must have been coming to the end of a world tour, perhaps not more than two or three centuries to go. My state of decay lends colour to this view, perhaps I had left my leg behind in the Pacific, yes, no perhaps about it, I had, somewhere off the coast of Java and its jungles red with rafflesia stinking of carrion, no, that's the Indian Ocean, what a gazetteer I am, no matter, somewhere round there. In a word I was returning to the fold, admittedly reduced, and doubtless fated to be even more so, before I could be restored to my wife and parents, you know, my loved ones, and clasp in my arms, both of which I had succeeded in preserving, my little ones born in my absence. I found myself in a kind of vast yard or campus, surrounded by high walls, its surface an amalgam of dirt and ashes, and this seemed sweet to me after the vast and heaving wastes I had traversed, if my information was correct. I almost felt out of danger! At the centre of this enclosure stood a

46

small rotunda, windowless, but well furnished with loopholes. Without being quite sure I had seen it before, I had been so long from home, I kept saying to myself, Yonder is the nest you should never have left, there your dear absent ones are awaiting your return, patiently, and you too must be patient. It was swarming with them, grandpa, grandma, little mother and the eight or nine brats. With their eyes glued to the slits and their hearts going out to me they surveyed my efforts. This yard so long deserted was now enlivened, for them, by me. So we turned, in our respective orbits, I without, they within. At night, keeping watch by turns, they observed me with the help of a searchlight. So the seasons came and went. The children increased in stature, the periods of Ptomaine grew pale, the ancients glowered at each other, muttering, to themselves, I'll bury you yet, or, You'll bury me yet. Since my arrival they had a subject of conversation, and even of discussion, the same as of old, at the moment of my setting forth, perhaps even an interest in life, the same as of old. Time hung less heavy on their hands. What about throwing him a few scraps? No no, it might upset him. They did not want to check the impetus that was sweeping me towards them. You wouldn't know him! True, papa, and yet you can't mistake him. They who in the ordinary way never answered when spoken to, my elders, my wife, she who had chosen me, rather

47

than one of her suitors. A few more summers and he'll be in our midst. Where am I going to put him? In the basement? Perhaps after all I am simply in the basement. What possesses him to be stopping all the time? Oh he was always like that, ever since he was a mite, always stopping, wasn't he, Granny? Yes indeed, never easy, always stopping. According to Mahood I never reached them, that is to say they all died first, the whole ten or eleven of them, carried off by sausage-poisoning, in great agony. Incommoded first by their shrieks, then by the stench of decomposition, I turned sadly away. But not so fast, otherwise we'll never arrive. It's no longer I in any case. He'll never reach us if he doesn't get a move on. He looks as if he had slowed down, since last year. Oh the last laps won't take him long. My missing leg didn't seem to affect them, perhaps it was already missing when I left. What about throwing him a sponge? No no, it might confuse him. In the evening, after supper, while my wife kept her eye on me, gaffer and gammer related my life history, to the sleepy children. Bedtime story atmosphere. That's one of Mahood's favourite tricks, to produce ostensibly independent testimony in support of my historical existence. The instalment over, all joined in a hymn, Safe in the arms of Jesus, for example, or, Jesus lover of my soul, let me to thy bosom fly, for example. Then they went to bed, with the exception of the one on

48

watch duty. My parents differed in their views on me, but they were agreed I had been a fine baby, at the very beginning, the first fortnight or three weeks. And yet he was a fine baby, with these words they invariably closed their relations. Often they fell silent, engulfed in their memories. Then it was usual for one of the children to launch, by way of envoy, the consecrated phrase, And yet he was a fine baby. A burst of clear and innocent laughter, from the mouths of those whom sleep had not yet overcome, greeted this premature conclusion. And the narrators themselves, torn from their melancholy thoughts, could scarce forbear to smile. Then they all rose, with the exception of my mother whose knees couldn't support her, and sang, Gentle Jesus, meek and mild, for example, or, Jesus, my one, my all, hear me when I call, for example. He too must have been a fine baby. Finally my wife announced the latest news, for them to take to bed with them. He's backing away again, or, He's stopped to scratch himself, or, You should have seen him hopping sidelong, or, Oh look children, quick he's down on his hands and knee, admittedly that must have been worth seeing. It was then customary that someone should ask her if I was approaching none the less, if in spite of everything I was making headway, they couldn't bear the thought of going to bed, those who were still awake, without the assurance that I wasn't losing ground. Ptoto set their minds at rest. I had moved, no further proof was needed. I had been drawing near for so long now that provided I remained in motion there could be no cause for anxiety. I was launched, there was no reason why I should suddenly begin to retreat, I just wasn't made that way. Then having kissed all round and wished one another happy dreams they retired, with the exception of the watch. What about hailing him? Poor Papa, he burned to encourage me vocally. Stick it, lad, it's your last winter. But in view of the trouble I was having, the trouble I was taking, they held him back, pointing out that the moment was ill-chosen to give me a shock. But what were my own feelings at this period? What was I thinking of? With what? Was I having difficulty with my morale? The answer to all that is this, I quote Malone, that I was entirely absorbed in the business on hand and not at all concerned to know precisely, or even approximately, what it consisted in. The only problem for me was how to continue, since I could not do otherwise, to the best of my declining powers, in the motion which had been imparted to me. This obligation, and the quasi-impossibility of fulfilling it, engrossed me in a purely mechanical way, excluding notably the free play of the intelligence and sensibility, so that my situation rather resembled that of an old broken-down cartor bat-horse unable to receive the least information either from its instinct or from its observation as to whether it is moving towards the stable or away from it, and not greatly caring either way. The question, among others, of how such things are possible had long since ceased to preoccupy me. This touching picture of my situation I found by no means unattractive and as I recall it I find myself wondering again if I was not in fact the creature revolving in that yard, as Mahood assured me. Well supplied with pain-killers I drew upon them freely, without however permitting myself the lethal dose that would have cut short my functions, whatever they may have been. Having somehow or other remarked the habitation and even admitted to myself that I had perhaps seen it before, I gave it no further thought, nor to the near and dear ones that filled it to overflowing, in a mounting fever of impatience. Though now close at hand, as the crow flies, to my goal, I did not quicken my step. I could have no doubt, but I had to husband my strength, if I was ever to arrive. I had no wish to arrive, but I had to do my utmost, in order to arrive. A desirable goal, no, I never had time to dwell on that. To go on, I still call that on, to go on and get on has been my only care, if not always in a straight line, at least in obedience to the figure assigned to me, there was never any room in my life for anything else. Still Mahood speaking. Never once have I stopped. My halts do not count. Their purpose was to enable me to go on. I did not use them to brood on my lot, but to rub myself as best I might with Elliman's Embrocation, for example, or to give myself an injection of laudanum, no easy matters for a man with only one leg. Often the cry went up, He's down! But in reality I had sunk to the ground of my own free will, in order to be rid of my crutches and have both hands available to minister to myself in peace and comfort. Admittedly it is difficult, for a man with but one leg, to sink to earth in the full force of the expression, particularly when he is weak in the head and the sole surviving leg flaccid for want of exercise, or from excess of it. The simplest thing then is to fling away the crutches and collapse. That is what I did. They were therefore right in saying I had fallen, they were not far wrong. Oh I have also been known to fall involuntarily, but not often, an old warrior like me, you can imagine. But have it any way you like. Up or down, taking my anodynes, waiting for the pain to abate, panting to be on my way again, I stopped, if you insist, but not in the sense they meant when they said, He's down again, he'll never reach us. When I penetrate into that house, if I ever do, it will be to go on turning, faster and faster, more and more convulsive, like a constipated dog, or one suffering from worms, overturning the furniture, in the midst of my family all trying to embrace me at once, until by virtue of a supreme spasm I am catapulted in the opposite direction and gradually leave backwards, without having said good-evening. I must really lend myself to this story a little longer, there may possibly be a grain of truth in it. Mahood must have remarked that I remained sceptical, for he casually let fall that I was lacking not only a leg, but an arm also. With regard to the homologous crutch, I seemed to have retained sufficient armpit to hold and manoeuvre it, with the help of my unique foot to kick the end of it forward as occasion required. But what shocked me profoundly, to such a degree that my mind (Mahood dixit) was assailed by insuperable doubts, was the suggestion that the misfortune experienced by my family and brought to my notice first by the noise of their agony, then by the smell of their corpses, had caused me to turn back. From that moment on I ceased to go along with him. I'll explain why, that will permit me to think of something else and in the first place of how to get back to me, back to where I am waiting for me, I'd just as soon not, but it's my only chance, at least I think so, the only chance I have of going silent, of saying something at last that is not false, if that is what they want, so as to have nothing more to say. My reasons. I'll give three or four, that ought to be enough for me. First this family of mine, the mere fact of having a family should have put me on my guard. But my good-will at certain moments is such, and my longing

53

to have floundered however briefly, however feebly, in the great life torrent streaming from the earliest proto-zoa to the very latest humans, that I, no, parenthesis unfinished. I'll begin again. My family. To begin with it had no part or share in what I was doing. Having set forth from that place, it was only natural I should return to it, given the accuracy of my navigation. And my family could have moved to other quarters during my absence, and settled down a hundred leagues away, without my deviating by as much as a hair's-breadth from my course. As for the screams of pain and wafts of decomposition, assuming I was capable of noticing them, they would have seemed to me quite in the natural order of things, such as I had come to know it. If before such manifestations I had been compelled each time to turn aside, I should not have got very far. Washed on the surface only by the rains, my head cracking with unutterable imprecations, it was from myself I should have had to turn aside, before all else. After all perhaps I was doing so, that would account for my vaguely circular motion. Lies, lies, mine was not to know, nor to judge, nor to rail, but to go. That the bacil-lus botulinus should have exterminated my entire kith and kin, I shall never weary of repeating this, was something I could readily admit, but only on condition that my personal behaviour had not to suffer by it. Let us rather consider what really took place, if Mahood was telling the truth. And why should he have lied to me, he so anxious to obtain my adhesion, to what now that I come to think of it, to his conception of me? Why? For fear of paining me perhaps. But I am there to be pained, that is what my tempters have never grasped. What they all wanted, each according to his particular notion of what is endurable, was that I should exist and at the same time be only moderately, or perhaps I should say finitely pained. They have even killed me off, with the friendly remark that having reached the end of my endurance I had no choice but to disappear. The end of my endurance! It was one second they should have schooled me to endure, after that I would have held out for all eternity, whistling a merry tune. The hard knocks they invented for me! But the bouquet was this story of Mahood's in which I appear as upset at having been delivered so economically of a pack of blood relations, not to mention the two cunts into the bargain, the one for ever accursed that ejected me into this world and the other, infundibuliform, in which, pumping my likes, I tried to take my revenge. To tell the truth, let us be honest at least, it is some considerable time now since I last knew what I was talking about. It is because my thoughts are elsewhere. I am therefore forgiven. So long as one's thoughts are somewhere everything is permitted. On then, without misgiving, as if nothing had happened.

And let us consider what really took place, if Mahood was telling the truth when he represented me as rid at one glorious sweep of parents, wife and heirs. I've plenty of time to blow it all skyhigh, this circus where it is enough to breathe to qualify for asphyxiation, I'll find a way out of it, it won't be like the other times. But I should not like to defame my defamer. For when he made me turn and set off in the other direction, before I had exhausted the possibilities of the one I was pursuing, he had not in mind a shrinking of the spirit, not for a moment, but a purely physiological commotion, followed by a simple desire to vomit, corresponding respectively to the howls of my family as they grudgingly succumbed and the subsequent stench, this latter compelling me to beat in retreat under penalty of losing consciousness entirely. This version of the facts having been restored, it only remains to say it is no better than the other and no less incompatible with the kind of creature I might just conceivably have been if they had known how to take me. So let us consider now what really occurred. Finally I found myself, without surprise, within the building, circular in form as already stated, its ground-floor consisting of a single room flush with the arena, and there completed my rounds, stamping under foot the unrecognisable remains of my family, here a face, there a stomach, as the case might be, and sinking into them with the ends of my crutches, both coming and going. To say I did so with satisfaction would be stretching the truth. For my feeling was rather one of annoyance at having to flounder in such muck just at the moment when my closing contortions called for a firm and level surface. I like to fancy, even if it is not true, that it was in mother's entrails I spent the last days of my long voyage, and set out on the next. No, I have no preference, Isolde's breast would have done just as well, or papa's private parts, or the heart of one of the little bastards. But is it certain? Would I have not been more likely, in a sudden access of independence, to devour what remained of the fatal corned-beef? How often did I fall during these final stages, while the storms raged without? But enough of this nonsense. I was never anywhere but here, no one ever got me out of here. Enough of acting the infant who has been told so often how he was found under a cabbage that in the end he remembers the exact spot in the garden and the kind of life he led there before joining the family circle. There will be no more from me about bodies and trajectories, sky and earth, I don't know what it all is. They have told me, explained to me, described to me, what it all is, what it looks like, what it's all for, one after the other, thousands of times, in thousands of connections, until I must have begun to look as if I understood. Who would ever think, to hear me, that I've never seen anything, never heard anything but their voices? And man, the lectures they gave me on men, before they even began trying to assimilate me to him! What I speak of, what I speak with, all comes from them. It's all the same to me, but it's no good, there's no end to it. It's of me now I must speak, even if I have to do it with their language, it will be a start, a step towards silence and the end of madness, the madness of having to speak and not being able to, except of things that don't concern me, that don't count, that I don't believe, that they have crammed me full of to prevent me from saying who I am, where I am, and from doing what I have to do in the only way that can put an end to it, from doing what I have to do. How they must hate me! Ah a nice state they have me in, but still I'm not their creature, not quite, not yet. To testify to them, until I die, as if there was any dying with that tomfoolery, that's what they've sworn they'll bring me to. Not to be able to open my mouth without proclaiming them, and our fellowship, that's what they imagine they'll have me reduced to. It's a poor trick that consists in ramming a set of words down your gullet on the principle that you can't bring them up without being branded as belonging to their breed. But I'll fix their gibberish for them. I never understood a word of it in any case, not a word of the stories it spews, like gobbets in a vomit. My inability to absorb, my genius for forgetting, are more than they reckoned with. Dear incomprehension, it's thanks to you I'll be myself, in the end. Nothing will remain of all the lies they have glutted me with. And I'll be myself at last, as a starveling belches his odourless wind, before the bliss of coma. But who, they? Is it really worth while inquiring? With my cogged means? No, but that's no reason not to. On their own ground, with their own arms, I'll scatter them, and their miscreated puppets. Perhaps I'll find traces of myself by the same occasion. That's decided then. What is strange is that they haven't been pestering me for some time past, yes, they've inflicted the notion of time on me too. What conclusion, using their methods, am I to draw from this? Mahood is silent, that is to say his voice continues, but is no longer renewed. Do they consider me so plastered with their rubbish that I can never extricate myself, never make a gesture but their cast must come to life? But within, motionless, I can live, and utter me, for no ears but my own. They loaded me down with their trappings and stoned me through the carnival. I'll sham dead now, whom they couldn't bring to life, and my monster's carapace will rot off me. But it's entirely a matter of voices, no other metaphor is appropriate. They've blown me up with their voices, like a balloon, and even as I collapse it's them I hear. Who, them? And why nothing more from them lately? Can it be they have abandoned me, saying, Very well, there's nothing to be done with him, let's leave it at that, he's not dangerous. Ah but the little murmur of unconsenting man, to murmur what it is their humanity stifles, the little gasp of the condemned to life, rotting in his dungeon garrotted and racked, to gasp what it is to have to celebrate banishment, beware. No, they have nothing to fear, I am walled round with their vociferations, none will ever know what I am, none will ever hear me say it, I won't say it, I can't say it, I have no language but theirs, no, perhaps I'll say it, even with their language, for me alone, so as not to have not lived in vain, and so as to go silent, if that is what confers the right to silence, and it's unlikely, it's they who have silence in their gift, they who decide, the same old gang, among themselves, no matter, to hell with silence, I'll say what I am, so as not to have not been born for nothing, I'll fix their jargon for them, then any old thing, no matter what, whatever they want, with a will, till time is done, at least with a good grace. First I'll say what I'm not, that's how they taught me to proceed, then what I am, it's already under way, I have only to resume at the point where I let myself be cowed. I am neither, I needn't say, Murphy, nor Watt, nor Mercier, nor – no, I can't even bring myself to name them, nor any of the others whose very names I forget, who told me I was they, who I must have tried to be, under duress, or through fear, or to avoid acknowledging me, not the slightest connection. I never desired, never sought, never suffered, never partook in any of that, never knew what it was to have, things, adversaries, mind, senses. But enough of this. There is no use denying, no use harping on the same old thing I know so well, and so easy to say, and which simply amounts in the end to speaking yet again in the way they intend me to speak, that is to say about them, even with execration and disbelief. Perhaps they exist in the way they have decreed will be mine, it's possible, I don't know and I'm not interested. If they had taught me how to wish I'd wish they did. There's no getting rid of them without naming them and their contraptions, that's the thing to keep in mind. I might as well tell another of Mahood's stories and no more about it, to be understood in the way I was given to understand it, namely as being about me. That's an idea. To heighten my disgust. I'll recite it. This will leave me free to consider how I may best proceed with my own affair, beginning again at the point where I had to interrupt it, under duress, or through fear, or through ignorance. It will be the last story. I'll try and look as if I was telling it willingly, to keep them quiet in case they should feel like refreshing my memory, on the subject of my behaviour above in the island, among my compatriots, contemporaries, coreligionists and companions in distress. This will leave me free to consider how to set about showing myself forth. No one will be any the wiser. But who are these maniacs let loose on me from on high for what they call my good, let us first try and throw a little light on that. To tell the truth – no, first the story. The island, I'm on the island, I've never left the island, God help me. I was under the impression I spent my life in spirals round the earth. Wrong, it's on the island I wind my endless ways. The island, that's all the earth I know. I don't know it either, never having had the stomach to look at it. When I come to the coast I turn back inland. And my course is not helicoidal, I got that wrong too, but a succession of irregular loops, now sharp and short as in the waltz, now of a parabolic sweep that embraces entire boglands, now between the two, somewhere or other, and invariably unpredictable in direction, that is to say determined by the panic of the moment. But at the period I refer to now this active life is at an end, I do not move and never shall again, unless it be under the impulsion of a third party. For of the great traveller I had been, on my hands and knees in the later stages, then crawling on my belly or rolling on the ground, only the trunk remains (in sorry trim), surmounted by the head with which we are already familiar, this is the part of myself the description of which I have best assimilated and retained. Stuck like a sheaf of flowers in a deep jar, its neck flush with my mouth, on the side of a quiet street near the shambles, I am at rest at last. If I turn, I shall not say my head, but my eyes, free to roll as they list, I can see the statue of the apostle of horse's meat, a bust. His pupilless eyes of stone are fixed upon me. That makes four, with those of my creator, omnipresent, do not imagine I flatter myself I am privileged. Though not exactly in order I am tolerated by the police. They know I am speechless and consequently incapable of taking unfair advantage of my situation to stir up the population against its governors, by means of burning oratory during the rush hour or subversive slogans whispered, after nightfall, to belated pedestrians the worse for drink. And since I have lost all my members, with the exception of the one-time virile, they know also that I shall not be guilty of any gestures liable to be construed as inciting to alms, a prisonable offence. The fact is I trouble no one, except possibly that category of hypersensitive persons for whom the least thing is an occasion for scandal and indignation. But even here the risk is negligible, such people avoiding the neighbourhood for fear of being overcome at the sight of the cattle, fat and fresh from their pastures, trooping towards the humane killer. From this point of view the spot is well chosen, from my point of view. And even those sufficiently unhinged to be affected by the spectacle I offer, I mean upset and temporarily diminished in their capacity for work and aptitude for happiness, need only look at me a second time, those who can bring themselves to do it, to have immediately their minds made easy. For my face reflects nothing but the satisfaction of one savouring a well-earned rest. It is true my mouth was hidden, most of the time, and my eyes closed. Ah yes, sometimes it's in the past, sometimes in the present. And alone perhaps the state of my skull, covered with pustules and bluebottles, these latter naturally abounding in such a neighbourhood, preserved me from being an object of envy for many, and a source of discontent. I hope this gives a fair picture of my situation. Once a week I was taken out of my receptacle, so that it might be emptied. This duty fell to the proprietress of the chop-house across the street and she performed it punctually and without complaint, beyond an occasional good-natured reflection to the effect that I was a nasty old pig, for she had a kitchen-garden. Without perhaps having exactly won her heart it was clear I did not leave her indifferent. And before putting me back she took advantage of the circumstance that my mouth was accessible to stick into it a chunk of lights or a marrowbone. And when snow fell she covered me with a tarpaulin still watertight in places. It was under its shelter, snug and dry, that I became acquainted with the boon of tears, while wondering to what I was indebted for it, not feeling moved. And this not merely once, but every time she covered me, that is to say twice or three times a year. Yes, it was fatal, no sooner had the tarpaulin settled over me, and the precipitate steps of my benefactress died away, than the tears began to flow. Is this, was this to be interpreted as an effect of gratitude? But in that case should not I have felt grateful? Besides I realised darkly that if she took care of me thus, it was not solely out of goodness, or else I had not rightly understood the meaning of goodness, when it was explained to me. It must not be forgotten that I represented for this woman an undeniable asset. For quite apart from the services I rendered to her lettuce, I constituted for her establishment a kind of landmark, not to say an advertisement, far more effective than for example a chef in cardboard, pot-bellied in profile and full face wafer thin. That she was well aware of this is shown by the trouble she had taken to festoon my jar with Chinese lanterns, of a very pretty effect in the twilight, and a fortiori in the night. And the jar itself, so that the passer-by might consult with greater ease the menu attached to it, had been raised on a pedestal at her own expense. It is thus I learnt that her turnips in gravy are not so good as they used to be, but that on the other hand her carrots, equally in gravy, are even better than formerly. The gravy has not varied. This is the kind of language I can almost understand, these the kind of clear and simple notions on which it is possible for me to build, I ask for no other spiritual nourishment. A turnip, I know roughly what a turnip is like, a carrot too, particularly the Flakkee, or Colmar Red. I seem to grasp at certain moments the nuance that divides bad from worse. And if I do not always feel the full force of yesterday and today, this does not detract very much from the satisfaction I feel at having penetrated the gist of the matter. Of her salad, for example, I never heard anything but praise. Yes, I represent for her a tidy little capital and, if I should ever happen to die, I am convinced she would be genuinely annoyed. This should help me to live. I like to fancy that when the fatal hour of reckoning comes, if it ever does, and my debt to nature is paid off at last, she will do her best to prevent the removal, from where it now stands, of the old vase in which I shall have accomplished my vicissitudes. And perhaps in the place now occupied by my head she will set a melon, or a vegetable-marrow, or a big pineapple with its little tuft, or better still, I don't know why, a swede, in memory of me. Then I shall not vanish quite, as is so often the way with people when buried. But it is not to speak of her that I have started lying again. *De nobis ipsis silemus*, decidedly that should have been my motto. Yes, they gave me some lessons in pigsty Latin too, it looks well, sprinkled through the perjury. It is perhaps worth noting that snow alone, provided of course it is heavy, entitles me to the tarpaulin. No other form of filthy weather lets loose in her the maternal instinct, in my favour. I have tried to make her understand, dashing my head angrily against the neck of the jar, that I should like to be shrouded more often. At the same time I let my spittle flow over, in an attempt to show my displeasure. In vain. I wonder what explanation she can have found to account for this behaviour. She must have talked it over with her husband and probably been told that I was merely stifling, that is just the reverse of the truth. But credit where credit is due, we made a balls of it between us, I with my signs and she with her reading of them. This story is no good, I'm beginning almost to believe it. But let us see how it is supposed to end, that will sober me. The trouble is I forget how it goes on. But did I ever know? Perhaps it stops there, perhaps they stopped it there, saying, who knows, There you are now, you don't need us any more. This in fact is one of their favourite devices, to stop suddenly at the least sign of adhesion from me, leaving me high and dry, with nothing for my renewal but the life they have imputed to me. And it is only when they see me stranded that they take up again the thread of my misfortunes, judging me still insufficiently vitalised to bring them to a successful conclusion alone. But instead of making the junction, I have often noticed this, I mean instead of resuming me at the point where I was left off, they pick me up at a much later stage, perhaps thereby hoping to induce in me the illusion that I had got through the interval all on my own, lived without help of any kind for quite some time, and with no recollection of by what means or in what circumstances, or even died, all on my own, and come back to earth again, by way of the vagina like a real live baby, and reached a ripe age, and even senility, without the least assistance from them and thanks solely to the hints they had given me. To saddle me with a lifetime is probably not enough for them, I have to be given a taste of two or three generations. But it's not certain. Perhaps all they have told me has reference to a single existence, the confusion of identities being merely apparent and due to my inaptitude to assume any. If I ever succeed in dying under my own steam, then they will be in a better position to decide if I am worthy to adorn another age, or to try the same one again, with the benefit of my experience. I may therefore perhaps legitimately suppose that the one-armed one-legged wayfarer of a moment ago and the wedge-headed trunk in which I am now marooned are simply two phases of the same carnal envelope, the soul being notoriously immune from deterioration and dismemberment. Having lost one leg, what indeed more likely than that I should mislay the other? And similarly for the arms. A natural transition in sum. But what then of that other old age they bestowed upon me, if I remember right, and that other middle age, when neither legs nor arms were lacking, but simply the power to profit by them? And of that kind of youth in which they had to give me up for dead? If I have a warm place, it is not in their hearts. Oh I don't say they haven't done all they could to be agreeable to me, to get me out of here, on no matter what pretext, in no matter what disguise. All I reproach them with is their insistence. For beyond them is that other who will not give me quittance until they have abandoned me as inutilisable and restored me to myself. Then at last I can set about saying what I was, and where, during all this long lost time. But who is he, if my guess is right, who is waiting for that, from me? And who these others whose designs are so different? And into whose hands I play when I ask myself such questions? But do I, do I? In the jar did I ask myself questions? And in the arena? I have dwindled, I dwindle. Not so long ago, with a kind of shrink of my head and shoulders, as when one is scolded, I could disappear. Soon, at my present rate of decrease, I may spare myself this effort. And spare myself the trouble of closing my eyes, so as not to see the day, for they are blinded by the jar a few inches away. And I have only to let my head fall forward against the wall to be sure that the light from above, which at night is that of the moon, will not be reflected there either, in those little blue mirrors, I used to look at myself in them, to try and brighten them. Wrong again, wrong again, this effort and this trouble will not be spared me. For the woman, displeased at seeing me sink lower and lower, has raised me up by filling the bottom of my jar with sawdust which she changes every week, when she makes my toilet. It is softer than the stone, but less hygienic. And I had got used to the stone. Now I'm getting used to the sawdust. It's an occupation. I could never bear to be idle, it saps one's energy. And I open and close my eyes, open and close, as in the past. And I move my head in and out, in and out, as heretofore. And often at dawn, having left it out all night, I bring it in, to mock the woman and lead her astray. For in the morning, when she has rattled up her shutters, the first look of her eyes still moist with fornication is for the jar. And when she does not see my head she comes running to find out what has happened. For either I have escaped during the night or else I have shrunk again. But just before she reaches me I up with it like a jack-in-the-box, the old eyes glaring up at her. I mentioned I cannot turn my head, and this is true, my neck having stiffened prematurely. But this does not mean it is always facing in the same direction. For with a kind of tossing and writhing I succeed in imparting to my trunk the degree of rotation required, and not merely in one direction, but in the other also. My little game, which I should have thought inoffensive, has cost me dear, and yet I could have sworn I was insolvable. It is true one does not know one's riches until they are lost and I probably have others still that only await the thief to be brought to my notice. And today, if I can still open and close my eyes, as in the past, I can no longer, because of my roguish character, move my head in and out, as in the good old days. For a collar, fixed to the mouth of the jar, now encircles my neck, just below the chin. And my lips which used to be hidden, and which I sometimes pressed against the freshness of the stone, can now be seen by all and sundry. Did I say I catch flies? I snap them up, clack! Does this mean I still have my teeth? To have lost one's limbs and preserved one's dentition, what a mockery! But to revert now to the gloomy side of this affair, I may say that this collar, or ring, of cement, makes it very awkward for me to turn, in the way I have said. I take advantage of this to learn to stay quiet. To have forever before my eyes, when I open them, approximately the same set of hallucinations exactly, is a joy I might never have known, but for my cang. There is really only one thing that worries me, and that is the prospect of being throttled if I should ever happen to shorten further. Asphyxia! I who was always the respiratory type, witness this thorax still mine, together with the abdomen. I who murmured, each time I breathed in, Here comes more oxygen, and each time I breathed out, There go the impurities, the blood is bright red again. The blue face! The obscene protrusion of the tongue! The tumefaction of the penis! The penis, well now, that's a nice surprise, I'd forgotten I had one. What a pity I have no arms, there might still be something to be wrung from it. No, 'tis better thus. At my age, to start manstuprating again, it would be indecent. And fruitless. And yet one can never tell. With a yo heave ho, concentrating with all my might on a horse's rump, at the moment when the tail rises, who knows, I might not go altogether empty-handed away. Heaven, I almost felt it flutter! Does this mean they did not geld me? I could have sworn they had gelt me. But perhaps I am getting mixed up with other scrota. Not another stir out of it in any case. I'll concentrate again. A Clydesdale. A Suffolk stallion. Come come, a little cooperation please, finish dying, it's the least you might do, after all the trouble they've taken to bring you to life. The worst is over. You've been sufficiently assassinated, sufficiently suicided, to be able now to stand on your own feet, like a big boy. That's what I keep telling myself. And I add, quite carried away, Slough off this mortal inertia, it is out of place, in this society. They can't do everything. They have put you on the right road, led you by the hand to the very brink of the precipice, now it's up to you, with an unassisted last step, to show them your gratitude. I like this colourful language, these bold metaphors and apostrophes. Through the splendours of nature they dragged a paralytic and now there's nothing more to admire it's my duty to jump, that it may be said, There goes another who has lived. It does not seem to occur to them that I was never there, that this glassy eye, this fallen chap and the foam at the mouth owe nothing to the Bay of Naples, or Aubervilliers. The last step! I who could never manage the first. But perhaps they would consider themselves sufficiently rewarded if I simply waited for the wind to blow me over. That by all means, it's in my repertory. The trouble is there is no wind equal to it. The cliff would have to cave in under me. If only I were alive inside one might look forward to heart-failure, or to a nice little infarctus somewhere or other. It's usually with sticks they put me out of their agony, the idea being to demonstrate, to the backers, and bystanders, that I had a beginning, and an end. Then planting the foot on my chest, where all is as usual, to the assembly, Ah if you had seen him fifty years ago, what push, what go! Knowing perfectly well they have to begin me all over again. But perhaps I exaggerate my need of them. I accuse myself of inertia, and yet I move, at least I did, can I by any chance have missed the tide? Let us consider the head. There something seems to stir, from time to time, no reason therefore to despair of a fit of apoplexy. What else? The organs of digestion and evacuation, though sluggish, are not wholly inactive, as is shown by the attentions I receive. It's encouraging. While there's life there's hope. The flies, considered as traumatic agents, hardly call for mention. I suppose they might bring me typhus. No, that's rats. I have seen a few, but they are not yet reduced to me. A lowly tapeworm? Not interesting. It is clear in any case that I have lost heart too lightly, it is quite possible I have all that is required to give them satisfaction. But already I'm beginning to be there no more, in that calamitous street they made so clear to me. I could describe it, I could have, a moment ago, as if I had been there, in the form they chose for me, diminished certainly, not the man I was, not much longer for this world, but the eyes still open to impressions, and one ear, sufficiently, and the head sufficiently obedient, to provide me at least with a vague idea of the elements to be eliminated from the setting in order for all to be empty and silent. That was always the way. Just at the moment when the world is assembled at last, and it begins to dawn on me how I can leave it, all fades and disappears. I shall never see this place again, where my jar stands on its pedestal, with its garland of many-coloured lanterns, and me inside it, I could not cling to it. Perhaps they will have me struck by lightning, for a change, or poleaxed, one merry bank-holiday evening, then bundled in my shroud and whisked away, out of sight and mind. Or removed alive, for a change, shifted and deposited elsewhere, on the off chance. And at my next appearance, if I ever appear again, all will be new, new and strange. But little by little I'll get used to it, admonished by them, used to the scene, used to me, and little by little the old problem will raise its horrid head, how to live, with their kind of life, for a single second, young or old, without aid and assistance. And thus reminded of other attempts, in other circumstances, I shall start asking myself questions, prompted by them, like those I have been asking, concerning me, and them, and these sudden shifts of time and age, and how to succeed at last where I had always failed, so that they may be pleased with me, and perhaps leave me in peace at last, and free to do what I have to do, namely try and please the other, if that is what I have to do, so that he may be pleased with me, and leave me in peace at last, and give me quittance, and the right to rest, and silence, if that is in his gift. It's a lot to expect of one creature, it's a lot to ask, that he should first behave as if he were not, then as if he were, before being admitted to that peace where he neither is, nor is not, and where the language dies that permits of such expressions. Two falsehoods, two trappings, to be borne to the end, before I can be let loose, alone, in the unthinkable unspeakable, where I have not ceased to be, where they will not let me be. It will perhaps be less restful than I appear to think, alone there at last, and never importuned. No matter, rest is one of their words, think is another. But here at last, it seems to me, is food for delirium. What a shame if I should pitch on something and never notice it, another candle throw its little light and I be none the wiser. Yes, I feel the moment has come for me to look back, if I can, and take my bearings, if I am to go on. If only I knew what I have been saying. Bah, no need to worry, it can only have been one thing, the same as ever. I have my faults, but changing my tune is not one of them. I have only to go on, as if there was something to be done, something begun, somewhere to go. It all boils down to a question of words, I must not forget this, I have not forgotten it. But I must have said this before, since I say it now. I have to speak in a certain way, with warmth perhaps, all is possible, first of the creature I am not, as if I were he, and then, as if I were he, of the creature I am. Before I can, etc. It's a question of voices, of voices to keep going, in the right manner, when they stop, on purpose, to put me to the test, as now the one whose burden is roughly to the effect that I am alive. Warmth, ease, conviction, the right manner, as if it were my own voice, pronouncing my own words, words pronouncing me alive, since that's how they want me to be, I don't know why, with their billions of quick, their trillions of dead, that's not enough for them, I too must contribute my little convulsion, mewl, howl, gasp and rattle, loving my neighbour and blessed with reason. But what is the right manner, I don't know. It is they who dictate this torrent of balls, they who stuffed me full of these groans that choke me. And out it all pours unchanged, I have only to belch to be sure of hearing them, the same old sour teachings I can't change a tittle of. A parrot, that's what they're up against, a parrot. If they had told me what I have to say, in order to meet with their approval, I'd be bound to say it, sooner or later. But God forbid, that would be too easy, my heart wouldn't be in it, I have to puke my heart out too, spew it up whole along with the rest of the vomit, it's then at last I'll look as if I mean what I'm saying, it won't be just idle words. Well, don't lose hope, keep your mouth open and your stomach turned, perhaps you'll come out with it one of these days. But the other voice, of him who does not share this passion for the animal kingdom, who is waiting to hear from me, what is its burden? Nice point, too nice for me. For on the subject of me properly so called, I know what I mean, so far as I know I have received no information up to date. May one speak of a voice, in these conditions? Probably not. And yet I do. The fact is all this business about voices requires to be revised, corrected and then abandoned. Hearing nothing I am none the less a prey to

77

communications. And I speak of voices! After all, why not, so long as one knows it's untrue. But there are limits, it appears. Let them come. So nothing about me. That is to say no connected statement. Faint calls, at long intervals. Hear me! Be yourself again! Someone has therefore something to say to me. But never the least news concerning me, beyond the insinuation that I am not in a condition to receive any, since I am not there, which I knew already. I have naturally remarked, in a moment of exceptional receptivity, that these exhortations are conveyed to me by the same channel as that used by Malone and Co. for their transports. That's suspicious, or rather would be if I still hoped to obtain, from these revelations to come, some truth of more value than those I have been plastered with ever since they took it into their heads I had better exist. But this fond hope, which buoyed me up as recently as a moment ago, if I remember right, has now passed from me. Two labours then, to be distinguished perhaps, as the mine from the quarry, on the plane of the effort required, but identically deficient in charm and interest. I. Who might that be? The galley-man, bound for the Pillars of Hercules, who drops his sweep under cover of night and crawls between the thwarts, towards the rising sun, unseen by the guard, praying for storm. Except that I've stopped praying for anything. No no, I'm still a suppliant. I'll get over it, between now and the last voyage, on this leaden sea. It's like the other madness, the mad wish to know, to remember, one's transgressions. I won't be caught at that again, I'll leave it to this year's damned. And now let us think no more about it, think no more about anything, think no more. He alone or they a many, all solicit me in the same tongue, the only one they taught me. They told me there were others, I don't regret not knowing them. The moment the silence is broken in this way it can only mean one thing. Orders, prayers, threats, praise, reproach, reasons. Praise, yes, they gave me to understand I was making progress. Well done, sonny, that will be all for today, run along now back to your dark and see you tomorrow. And there I am, with my white beard, sitting among the children, babbling, cringing from the rod. I'll die in the lower third, bowed down with years and impositions, four foot tall again, like when I had a future, bare-legged in my old black pinafore, wetting my drawers. Pupil Mahood, for the twenty-five thousandth time, what is a mammal? And I'll fall down dead, worn out by the rudiments. But I'll have made progress, they told me so, only not enough, not enough. Ah! Where was I, in my lessons? That is what has had a fatal effect on my development, my lack of memory, no doubt about it. Pupil Mahood, repeat after me, Man is a higher mammal. I couldn't. Always talking about mammals, in this menagerie.

79

Frankly, between ourselves, what the hell could it matter to pupil Mahood, that man was this rather than that? Presumably nothing has been lost in any case, since here it all comes slobbering out again, let loose by the nightmare. I'll have my bellyful of mammals, I can see that from here, before I wake. Quick, give me a mother and let me suck her white, pinching my tits. But it's time I gave this solitary a name, nothing doing without proper names. I therefore baptise him Worm. It was high time. Worm. I don't like it, but I haven't much choice. It will be my name too, when the time comes, when I needn't be called Mahood any more, if that happy time ever comes. Before Mahood there were others like him, of the same breed and creed, armed with the same prong. But Worm is the first of his kind. That's soon said. I must not forget I don't know him. Perhaps he too will weary, renounce the task of forming me and make way for another, having laid the foundations. He has not yet been able to speak his mind, only murmur, I have not ceased to hear his murmur, all the while the others discoursed. He has survived them all, Mahood too, if Mahood is dead. I can hear him yet, faithful, begging me to still this dead tongue of the living. I imagine that is what he says, in his unchanging tone. If I could be silent I would better understand what he wants of me, wants me to be, wants me to say. Why doesn't he thunder it at me and get it over? Too easy, it is I who must be silent, hold my breath. But there is something wrong here. For if Mahood were silent, Worm would be silent too. That the impossible should be asked of me, good, what else could be asked of me? But the absurd! Of me whom they have reduced to reason. It is true poor Worm is not to blame for this. That's soon said. But let me complete my views, before I shit on them. For if I am Mahood, I am Worm too, plop. Or if I am not yet Worm, I shall be when I cease to be Mahood, plop. On now to serious matters. No, not yet. Another of Mahood's yarns perhaps, to perfect my besotment. No, not worth the trouble, it will come at its appointed hour, the record is in position from time immemorial. Yes, the big words must out too, all be taken as it comes. The problem of liberty too, as sure as fate, will come up for my consideration at the pre-established moment. But perhaps I have been too hasty in opposing these two fomenters of fiasco. Is it not the fault of one that I cannot be the other? Accomplices therefore. That's the way to reason, warmly. Or is one to postulate a tertius gaudens, meaning myself, responsible for the double failure? Shall I come upon my true countenance at last, bathing in a smile? I have the feeling I shall be spared this spectacle. At no moment do I know what I'm talking about, nor of whom, nor of where, nor how, nor why, but I could employ fifty wretches for this sinister operation and still be short of a fifty-first, to close the circuit, that I know, without knowing what it means. The essential is never to arrive anywhere, never to be anywhere, neither where Mahood is, nor where Worm is, nor where I am, it little matters thanks to what dispensation. The essential is to go on squirming forever at the end of the line, as long as there are waters and banks and ravening in heaven a sporting God to plague his creature, per pro his chosen shits. I've swallowed three hooks and am still hungry. Hence the howls. What a joy to know where one is, and where one will stay, without being there. Nothing to do but stretch out comfortably on the rack, in the blissful knowledge you are nobody for all eternity. A pity I should have to give tongue at the same time, it prevents it from bleeding in peace, licking the lips. Well I suppose one can't have everything, so late in the proceedings. They'll surely bring me to the surface one day or another and all then sink their differences and agree it was not worth while going to so much trouble for such a paltry kill, for such paltry killers. What silence then! And now let's see what news there is of Worm, just to please the old bastard. I'll soon know if the other is still after me. But even if he isn't nothing will come of it, he won't catch me, I won't be delivered from him, I mean Worm, I swear it, the other never caught me, I was never delivered from him, it's past history, up to the present. I am he who will never be caught, never delivered, who crawls between the thwarts, towards the new day that promises to be glorious, festooned with lifebelts, praying for rack and ruin. The third line falls plumb from the skies, it's for her majesty my soul, I'd have hooked her on it long ago if I knew where to find her. That brings us up to four, gathered together. I knew it, there might be a hundred of us and still we'd lack the hundred and first, we'll always be short of me. Worm, I nearly said Watt, Worm, what can I say of Worm, who hasn't the wit to make himself plain, what to still this gnawing of termites in my Punch and Judy box, what that might not just as well be said of the other? Perhaps it's by trying to be Worm that I'll finally succeed in being Mahood, I hadn't thought of that. Then all I'll have to do is be Worm. Which no doubt I shall achieve by trying to be Jones. Then all I'll have to do is be Jones. Stop, perhaps he'll spare me that, have compassion and let me stop. The dawn will not be always rosy. Worm, Worm, it's between the three of us now, and the devil take the hindmost. It seems to me besides that I must have already made, contrary to what it seems to me I must have already said, some efforts in this direction. I should have noted them, if only in my head. But Worm cannot note. There at least is a first affirmation, I mean negation, on which to build. Worm cannot note. Can Mahood note? That's it, weave, weave. Yes, it is the characteristic, among others, of

Mahood to note, even if he does not always succeed in doing so, certain things, perhaps I should say all things, so as to turn them to account, for his governance. And indeed we have seen him do so, in the yard, in his jar, in a sense. I knew I had only to try and talk of Worm to begin talking of Mahood, with more felicity and understanding than ever. How close to me he suddenly seems, squinting up at the medals of the hippophagist Ducroix. It is the hour of the apéritif, already people pause, to read the menu. Charming hour of the day, particularly when, as sometimes happens, it is also that of the setting sun whose last rays, raking the street from end to end, lend to my cenotaph an interminable shadow, astraddle of the gutter and the sidewalk. There was a time I used to contemplate it, when I was freer to turn my head than now, since being put in the collar. Then over there, far from me, I knew my head was lying, and people treading on it, and on my flies, which went on gliding none the less, prettily on the dark ground. And I saw the people coming towards me, all along my shadow, followed by long faithful trembling shadows. For sometimes I confuse myself with my shadow, and sometimes don't. And sometimes I don't confuse myself with my jar, and sometimes do. It all depends what mood we're in. And often I went on looking without flinching until, ceasing to be, I ceased to see. Delicious instant truly, coinciding from time to time, as already observed, with that of the apéritif. But this joy, which for my part I should have thought harmless, and without danger for the public, is something I have to go without now that the collar holds my face turned towards the railings, just above the menu, for it is important that the prospective customer should be able to compose his meal without the risk of being run over. The meat, in this quarter, has a high reputation, and people come from a distance, from great distances, on purpose to relish it. Which having done they hurry away. By ten o'clock in the evening all is silent, as the grave, as they say. Such is the fruit of my observations accumulated over a long period of years and constantly subjected to a process of induction. Here all is killing and eating. This evening there is tripe. It's a winter dish, or a late autumn one. Soon Marguerite will come and light me up. She is late. Already more than one passer-by has flashed his lighter under my nose the better to decipher what I shall now describe, by way of elegant variation, as the bill of fare. Please God nothing has happened to my protectress. I shall not hear her coming, I shall not hear her steps, because of the snow. I spent all morning under my cover. When the first frosts come she makes me a nest of rags, well tucked in all round me, to preserve me from chills. It's snug. I wonder will she powder my skull this evening, with her great puff. It's her latest invention. She's always

85

thinking of something new, to relieve me. If only the earth would quake! The shambles swallow me up! Through the railings, at the end of a vista between two blocks of buildings, the sky appears to me. A bar moves over and shuts it off, whenever I please. If I could raise my head I'd see it streaming into the main of the firmament. What is there to add, to these particulars? The evening is still young, I know that, don't let us go just yet, not yet say goodbye once more forever, to this heap of rubbish. What about trying to cogitate, while waiting for something intelligible to take place? Just this once. Almost immediately a thought presents itself, I should really concentrate more often. Quick let me record it before it vanishes. How is it the people do not notice me? I seem to exist for none but Madeleine. That a passer-by pressed for time, in headlong flight or hot pursuit, should have no eyes for me, that I can conceive. But the idlers come to hear the cattle's bellows of pain and who, time obviously heavy on their hands, pace up and down waiting for the slaughter to begin? The hungry compelled by the position of the menu, and whether they like it or not, to post themselves literally face to face with me, in the full blast of my breath? The children on their way to and from their playgrounds beyond the gates, all out for a bit of fun? It seems to me that even a human head, recently washed and with a few hairs on top, should be quite a popular curiosity in the position occupied by mine. Can it be out of discretion, and a reluctance to hurt, that they affect to be unaware of my existence? But this is a refinement of feeling which can hardly be attributed to the dogs that come pissing against my abode, apparently never doubting that it contains some flesh and bones. It follows therefore that I have no smell either. And yet if anyone should have a smell, it is I. How, under these conditions, can Mahood expect me to behave normally? The flies vouch for me, if you like, but how far? Would they not settle with equal appetite on a lump of cowshit? No, as long as this point is not cleared up to my satisfaction, or as long as I am not distinguished by some sense organs other than Madeleine's, it will be impossible for me to believe, sufficiently to pursue my act, the things that are told about me. I should further remark, with regard to this testimony which I consider indispensable, that I shall soon be in no fit condition to receive it, so greatly have my faculties declined, in recent times. It is obvious we have here a principle of change pregnant with possibilities. But say I succeed in dying, to adopt the most comfortable hypothesis, without having been able to believe I ever lived, I know to my cost it is not that they wish for me. For it has happened to me many times already, without their having granted me as much as a brief sick-leave among the worms, before resurrecting me. But who knows, this time, what the future holds in store. That qua sentient and thinking being I should be going downhill fast is in any case an excellent thing. Perhaps some day some gentleman, chancing to pass my way with his sweetheart on his arm, at the precise moment when my last is favouring me with a final smack of the flight of time, will exclaim, loud enough for me to hear, Oh I say, this man is ailing, we must call an ambulance! Thus with a single stone, when all hope seemed lost, the two rare birds. I shall be dead, but I shall have lived. Unless one is to suppose him victim of a hallucination. Yes, to dispel all doubt his betrothed would need to say, You are right, my love, he looks as if he were going to throw up. Then I'd know for certain and giving up the ghost be born at last, to the sound perhaps of one of those hiccups which mar alas too often the solemnity of the passing. When Mahood I once knew a doctor who held that scientific-ally speaking the latest breath could only issue from the fundament and this therefore, rather than the mouth, the orifice to which the family should present the mirror, before opening the will. However this may be, and without dwelling further on these macabre details, it is certain I was grievously mistaken in sup-posing that death in itself could be regarded as evidence, or even a strong presumption, in support of a preliminary life. And I for my part have no longer the

88

least desire to leave this world, in which they keep trying to foist me, without some kind of assurance that I was really there, such as a kick in the arse, for example, or a kiss, the nature of the attention is of little importance, provided I cannot be suspected of being its author. But let two third parties remark me, there, before my eyes, and I'll take care of the rest. How all becomes clear and simple when one opens an eye on the within, having of course previously exposed it to the without, in order to benefit by the contrast. I should be sorry, though exhausted personally, to abandon prematurely this rich vein. For I shall not come back to it in a hurry, ah no. But enough of this cursed first person, it is really too red a herring, I'll get out of my depth if I'm not careful. But what then is the subject? Mahood? No, not yet. Worm? Even less. Bah, any old pronoun will do, provided one sees through it. Matter of habit. To be adjusted later. Where was I? Ah yes, the bliss of what is clear and simple. The next thing is somehow to connect this with the unhappy Madeleine and her great goodness. Attentions such as hers, the pertinacity with which she continues to acknowledge me, do not these sufficiently attest my real presence here, in the Rue Brancion, never heard of in my island home? Would she rid me of my paltry excrements every Sunday, make me a nest at the approach of winter, protect me from the snow, change my sawdust, rub salt into my scalp, I hope I'm not forgetting anything, if I were not there? Would she have put me in a cang, raised me on a pedestal, hung me with lanterns, if she were not convinced of my substantiality? How happy I should be to submit to this evidence and to the execution upon me of the sentence it entails. Unfortunately I regard it as highly subject to caution, not to say unallowable. For what is one to think of the redoubled attentions she has been lavishing on me for some time past? How different from the serenity of our early relations, when I saw her only once a week. No, there is no getting away from it, this woman is losing faith in me. And she is trying to put off the moment when she must finally confess her error by coming every few minutes to see if I am still more or less imaginable in situ. Similarly the belief in God, in all modesty be it said, is sometimes lost following a period of intensified zeal and observance, it appears. Here I pause to make a distinction (I must be still thinking). That the jar is really standing where they say, all right, I wouldn't dream of denying it, after all it's none of my business, though its presence at such a place, about the reality of which I do not propose to quibble either, does not strike me as very credible. No, I merely doubt that I am in it. It is easier to raise a shrine than bring the deity down to haunt it. But what's all this confusion now? That's what comes of distinctions. No matter. She loves me, I've always felt it. She needs me. Her chop-house, her husband, her children if she has any, are not enough, there is in her a void that I alone can fill. It is not surprising then she should have visions. There was a time I thought she was perhaps a near relation, mother, sister, daughter, or such-like, perhaps even a wife, and that she was sequestrating me. That is to say Mahood, seeing how little impressed I was by his chief witness, whispered this suggestion in my ear, adding, I didn't say anything. I must admit it is not so preposterous as it looks at first sight, it even accounts for certain bizarreries which had not yet struck me at the time of its formulation, among others my inexistence in the eyes of those who are not in the know, that is to say all mankind. But assuming I was being stowed away in a public place, why go to such trouble to draw attention to my head, artistically illuminated from dusk to midnight? You may of course retort that results are all that count. Another thing however. This woman has never spoken to me, to the best of my knowledge. If I have said anything to the contrary I was mistaken. If I say anything to the contrary again I shall be mistaken again. Unless I am mistaken now. Into the dossier with it in any case, in support of whatever thesis you fancy. Never an affectionate word, never a reprimand. For fear of bringing me to the public notice? Or lest the illusion should be dispelled? I shall now sum up. The moment is at hand when my only believer must deny me. Nothing has happened. The lanterns have not been lit. Is it the same evening? Perhaps dinner is over. Perhaps Marguerite has come and gone, come again and gone again, without my having noticed her. Perhaps I have blazed with all my usual brilliance, for hours on end, all unsuspecting. And yet something has changed. It is not a night like other nights. Not because I see no stars, it is not often I see a star, away up in the depths of the sliver of sky I command. Not because I don't see anything, not even the railings, that has often happened. Not because of the silence either, it is a silent place, at night. And I am half-deaf. It is not the first time I have strained my ears in vain for the stables' muffled sounds. All of a sudden a horse will neigh. Then I'll know that nothing has changed. Or I'll see the lantern of the watchman, swinging knee-high in the yard. I must be patient. It is cold, this morning it snowed. And yet I don't feel the cold on my head. Perhaps I am still under the tarpaulin, perhaps she flung it over me again, for fear of more snow in the night, while I was meditating. But the sensation I so love, of the tarpaulin weighing on my head, is lacking too. Has my head lost all feeling? Or did I have a stroke, while I was meditating? I don't know. I shall be patient, asking no more questions, on the qui vive. Hours have passed, it must be day again, nothing has happened, I hear nothing. I placed them before their responsibilities, perhaps they have let me go. For this feeling of being entirely enclosed, and yet nothing touching me, is new. The sawdust no longer presses against my stumps, I don't know where I end. I left it yesterday, Mahood's world, the street, the chop-house, the slaughter, the statue and, through the railings, the sky like a slate-pencil. I shall never hear again the lowing of the cattle, nor the clinking of the forks and glasses, nor the angry voices of the butchers, nor the litany of the dishes and the prices. There will never be another woman wanting me in vain to live, my shadow at evening will not darken the ground. The stories of Mahood are ended. He has realised they could not be about me, he has abandoned, it is I who win, who tried so hard to lose, in order to please him, and be left in peace. Having won, shall I be left in peace? It doesn't look like it, I seem to be going on talking. In any case all these suppositions are probably erroneous. I shall no doubt be launched again, girt with better arms, against the fortress of mortality. What is more important is that I should know what is going on now, in order to announce it, as my function requires. It must not be forgotten, sometimes I forget, that all is a question of voices. I say what I am told to say, in the hope that some day they will weary of talking at me. The trouble is I say it wrong, having no ear, no head, no memory.

Now I seem to hear them say it is Worm's voice beginning, I pass on the news, for what it is worth. Do they believe I believe it is I who am speaking? That's theirs too. To make me believe I have an ego all my own, and can speak of it, as they of theirs. Another trap to snap me up among the living. It's how to fall into it they can't have explained to me sufficiently. They'll never get the better of my stupidity. Why do they speak to me thus? Is it possible certain things change on their passage through me, in a way they can't prevent? Do they believe I believe it is I who am asking these questions? That's theirs too, a little distorted perhaps. I don't say it's not the right method. I don't say they won't catch me in the end. I wish they would, to be thrown away. It's this hunt that is tiring, this unending being at bay. Images, they imagine that by piling on the images they'll entice me in the end. Like the mother who whistles to prevent baby's bladder from bursting, there's another. They, yes, now they're all in the same galley. Worm to play, his lead, I wish him a happy time. To think I thought he was against what they were trying to do with me! To think I saw in him, if not me, a step towards me! To get me to be he, the anti-Mahood, and then to say, But what am I doing but living, in a kind of way, the only possible way, that's the combination. Or by the absurd prove to me that I am, the absurd of not being able. Unfortunately it is no

94

help my being forewarned, I never remain so for long. In any case I wish him every success, in his courageous undertaking. And I am even prepared to collaborate with him, as with Mahood and Co., to the best of my ability, being unable to do otherwise, and knowing my ability. Worm, to say he does not know what he is, where he is, what is happening, is to underestimate him. What he does not know is that there is anything to know. His senses tell him nothing, nothing about himself, nothing about the rest, and this distinction is beyond him. Feeling nothing, knowing nothing, he exists nevertheless, but not for himself, for others, others conceive him and say, Worm is, since we conceive him, as if there could be no being but being conceived, if only by the beer. Others. One alone, then others. One alone turned towards the all-impotent, all-nescient, that haunts him, then others. Towards him whom he would nourish, he the famished one, and who, having nothing human, has nothing else, has nothing, is nothing. Come into the world unborn, abiding there unliving, with no hope of death, epi-centre of joys, of griefs, of calm. Who seems the truest possession, because the most unchanging. The one outside of life we always were in the end, all our long vain life long. Who is not spared by the mad need to speak, to think, to know where one is, where one was, during the wild dream, up above, under the skies, venturing forth at night. The one ignorant of himself and silent, ignorant of his silence and silent, who could not be and gave up trying. Who crouches in their midst who see themselves in him and in their eyes stares his unchanging stare. Thanks for these first notions. And it's not all. He who seeks his true countenance, let him be of good cheer, he'll find it, convulsed with anguish, the eyes out on stalks. He who longs to have lived, while he was alive, let him be reassured, life will tell him how. That's all very comforting. Worm, be Worm, you'll see, it's impossible, what a velvet glove, a little worn at the knuckles with all the hard hitting. Bah, let's turn the black eye. And the starching begin at last, of this old clout so patiently pawed in vain, as limp and drooping still as the first day. But it is solely a question of voices, no other image is appropriate. Let it go through me at last, the right one, the last one, his who has none, by his own confession. Do they think they'll lull me, with all this hemming and hawing? What can it matter to me, that I succeed or fail? The undertaking is none of mine, if they want me to succeed I'll fail, and vice versa, so as not to be rid of my tormentors. Is there a single word of mine in all I say? No, I have no voice, in this matter I have none. That's one of the reasons why I confused myself with Worm. But I have no reasons either, no reason, I'm like Worm, without voice or reason, I'm Worm, no, if I were Worm I wouldn't know it, I wouldn't say it, I wouldn't say anything, I'd be Worm. But I don't say anything, I don't know anything, these voices are not mine, nor these thoughts, but the voices and thoughts of the devils who beset me. Who make me say that I can't be Worm, the inexpugnable. Who make me say that I am he perhaps, as they are. Who make me say that since I can't be he I must be he. That since I couldn't be Mahood, as I might have been, I must be Worm, as I cannot be. But is it still they who say that when I have failed to be Worm I'll be Mahood, automatically, on the rebound? As if, and a little silence, as if I were big enough now to take a hint and understand, certain things, but they're wrong, I need explanations, of everything, and even then, I don't understand, that's how I'll sicken them in the end, by my stupidity, so they say, to lull me, to make me think I'm stupider than I am. And is it still they who say that when I surprise them all and am Worm at last, then at last I'll be Mahood, Worm proving to be Mahood the moment one is he? Ah if they could only begin, and do what they want with me, and succeed at last, in doing what they want with me, I'm ready to be whatever they want, I'm tired of being matter, matter, pawed and pummelled endlessly in vain. Or give me up and leave me lying in a heap, in such a heap that none would ever be found again to try and fashion it. But they are not of the same mind, they are all of the same kidney and yet they don't know what they want to do with me, they don't know where I am, or what I'm like, I'm like dust, they want to make a man out of dust. Listen to them, losing heart! That's to lull me, till I imagine I hear myself saying, myself at last, to myself at last, that it can't be they, speaking thus, that it can only be I, speaking thus. Ah if I could only find a voice of my own, in all this babble, it would be the end of their troubles, and of mine. That's why there are all these little silences, to try and make me break them. They think I can't bear silence, that some day, somehow, my horror of silence will force me to break it. That's why they are always leaving off, to try and drive me to extremities. But they dare not be silent for long, the whole fabrication might collapse. It's true I dread these gulfs they all bend over, straining their ears for the murmur of a man. It isn't silence, it's pit-falls, into which nothing would please me better than to fall, with the little cry that might be taken for human, like a wounded wistiti, the first and last, and vanish for good and all, having squeaked. Well, if they ever succeed in getting me to give a voice to Worm, in a moment of euphory, perhaps I'll succeed in making it mine, in a moment of confusion. There we have the stake. But they won't. Did they ever get Mahood to speak? It seems to me not. I think Murphy spoke now and then, the others too perhaps, I don't remember, but it was clumsily done, you could see the ventriloquist. And now I feel it's about to begin. They must consider me sufficiently stupefied, with all their balls about being and existing. Yes, now that I've forgotten who Worm is, where he is, what he's like, I'll begin to be he. Anything rather than these college quips. Quick, a place. With no way in, no way out, a safe place. Not like Eden. And Worm inside. Feeling nothing, knowing nothing, capable of nothing, wanting nothing. Until the instant he hears the sound that will never stop. Then it's the end, Worm no longer is. We know it, but we don't say it, we say it's the awakening, the beginning of Worm, for now we must speak, and speak of Worm. It's no longer he, but let us proceed as if it were still he, he at last, who hears, and trembles, and is delivered over, to affliction and the struggle to withstand it, the starting eye, the labouring mind. Yes, let us call that thing Worm, so as to exclaim, the sleight of hand accomplished, Oh look, life again, life everywhere and always, the life that's on every tongue, the only possible! Poor Worm, who thought he was different, there he is in the madhouse for life. Where am I? That's my first question, after an age of listening. From it, when it hasn't been answered, I'll rebound towards others, of a more personal nature, much later. Perhaps I'll even end up, before regaining my coma, by thinking of myself as living, technically speaking. But let us proceed with method. I shall do my best, as always, since I cannot do otherwise. I shall submit, more corpse-obliging than ever. I shall transmit the words as received, by the ear, or roared through a trumpet into the arsehole, in all their purity, and in the same order, as far as possible. This infinitesimal lag, between arrival and departure, this trifling delay in evacuation, is all I have to worry about. The truth about me will boil forth at last, scalding, provided of course they don't start stuttering again. I listen. Enough procrastination. I'm Worm, that is to say I am no longer he, since I hear. But I'll forget that in the heat of misery, I'll forget I am no longer Worm, but a kind of tenth-rate Toussaint L'Ouverture, that's what they're counting on. Worm then I catch this sound that will never stop, monotonous beyond words and yet not altogether devoid of a certain variety. At the end of I know not what eternity, they don't say, this has sufficiently exasperated my intelligence for it to grasp that the nuisance is a voice and that the realm of nature, in which I flatter myself I have a foot already, has other noises to offer which are even more unpleasant and may be relied on to make themselves heard before long. Don't tell me after that I had no predispositions for man's estate. What a weary way since that first disaster, what nerves torn from the heart of insentience, with the appertaining terror and the cerebellum on fire. It took him a long time to adapt himself to this

excoriation. To realise pooh it's nothing. A mere baga-
telle. The common lot. A harmless joke. That will not
last for ever. For me to gather while I may. They mentioned roses. I'll smell them before I'm finished. Then
they'll put the accent on the thorns. What prodigious
variety! The thorns they'll have to come and stick into
me, as into their unfortunate Jesus. No, I need nobody,
they'll start sprouting under my arse, unaided, some
day I feel myself soaring above my condition. A billy-
bowl of thorns and the air perfume-laden. But not so
fast. I still leave much to be desired, I have no technique, none. For example, in case you don't believe
me, I don't yet know how to move, either locally, in
relation to myself, or bodily, in relation to the rest of
the shit. I don't know how to want to, I want to in vain.
What doesn't come to me from me has come to the
wrong address. Similarly my understanding is not yet
sufficiently well-oiled to function without the pressure
of some critical circumstance, such as a violent pain felt
for the first time. Some nice point in semantics, for
example, of a nature to accelerate the march of the
hours, could not retain my attention. For others the
time-abolishing joys of impersonal and disinterested
speculation. I only think, if that is the name for this
vertiginous panic as of hornets smoked out of their
nest, once a certain degree of terror has been exceeded.
Does this mean I am less exposed to doing so, by the

grace of inurement? To argue so would be to under-estimate the extent of the repertory in which I am plunged and which, it appears, is nothing compared to what is in store for me at the conclusion of the novitiate. These lights gleaming low afar, then rearing up in a blaze and sweeping down upon me, blinding, to devour me, are merely one example. My familiarity with them avails me nothing, they invariably give me to reflect. Each time, at the last moment, just as I begin to scorch, they go out, smoking and hissing, and yet each time my phlegm is shattered. And in my head, which I am beginning to locate to my satisfaction, above and a little to the right, the sparks spirt and dash themselves out against the walls. And sometimes I say to myself I am in a head, it's terror makes me say it, and the longing to be in safety, surrounded on all sides by massive bone. And I add that I am foolish to let myself be frightened by another's thoughts, lacerating my sky with harmless fires and assailing me with noises signifying nothing. But one thing at a time. And often all sleeps, as when I was really Worm, except this voice which has denatured me, which never stops, but often grows confused and falters, as if it were going to abandon me. But it is merely a passing weakness, unless it is done on purpose, to teach me hope. Strange thing, ruined as I am and still young in this abjection they have brought me to, I sometimes seem to remember what I was like when I was Worm, and not yet delivered into their hands. That's to tempt me into saying, I am indeed Worm after all, and into thinking that after all he may have become the thing that I have become. But it doesn't work. But they will devise another means, less childish, of getting me to admit, or pretend to admit, that I am he whose name they call me by, and no other. Or they'll wait, counting on my weariness, as they press me ever harder, to wipe him from my memory who cannot be brought to the pass they have brought me to, not to mention yesterday, not to mention tomorrow. And yet it seems to me I remember, and shall never forget, what I was like when I was he, before all became confused. But that is of course impossible, since Worm could not know what he was like, or who he was, that's how they want me to reason. And it seems to me too, which is even more deplorable, that I could become Worm again, if I were left in peace. This transmission is really excellent. I wonder if it's going to get us somewhere. If only they would stop talking for nothing, pending their stopping everything. Nothing? That's soon said. It is not for me to judge. What would I judge with? It's more provocation. They want me to lose patience and rush, suddenly beside myself, to their rescue. How transparent that all is! Sometimes I say to myself, they say to me, Worm says to me, the subject matters little, that my purveyors are more than one, four or five. But it's more likely the same foul brute all the time, amusing himself pretending to be a many, varying his register, his tone, his accent and his drivel. Unless it comes natural to him. A bare and rusty hook I might accept. But all these titbits! But there are long silences too, at long intervals, during which, hearing nothing, I say nothing. That is to say I hear murmuring, if I listen hard enough, but it's not for me, it's for them alone, they are putting their heads together again. I don't hear what they say, all I know is they are still there, they haven't done, with me. They have moved a little aside. Secrets. Or if there is only one it is he alone, taking counsel with himself, muttering and chewing his moustache, getting ready for a fresh flow of inanity. To think of me eavesdropping, me, when silence falls! Ah a nice state they have me in. But it's with the hope there is no one left. But this is not the time to speak of that. Good. Of what is it the time to speak? Of Worm, at last. Good. We must first, to begin with, go back to his beginnings and then, to go on with, follow him patiently through the various stages, taking care to show their fatal concatenation, which have made him what I am. The whole to be tossed off with bravura. Then notes from day to day, until I collapse. And finally, to wind up with, song and dance of thanksgiving by victim, to celebrate his nativity. Please God nothing goes wrong. Mahood I couldn't die. Worm will I ever get born? It's the same problem. But perhaps not the same personage after all. The scytheman will tell, it's all one to him. But let us go back as planned, afterwards we'll fall forward as projected. The reverse would be more like it. But not by much. Upstream, downstream, what matter, I begin by the ear, that's the way to talk. Before that it was the night of time. Whereas ever since, what radiance! Now at least I know where I am, as far as my origins go, I mean my origins considered as a subject of conversation, that's what counts. The moment one can say, Someone is on his way, all is well. Perhaps I have still a thousand years to go. No matter. He's on his way. I begin to be familiar with the premises. I wonder if I couldn't sneak out by the fundament, one morning, with the French breakfast. No, I can't move, not yet. One minute in a skull and the next in a belly, strange, and the next nowhere in particular. Perhaps it's Botal's Foramen, when all about me palpitates and labours. Bait, bait. Can it be I have a friend among them, shaking his head in sorrow and saying nothing or only, from time to time, Enough, enough. One can be before beginning, they have set their hearts on that. They want me roots and all. This onward-rushing time is the same which used to sleep. And this silence they yelp against in vain and which one day will be restored, the same as in the past. Perhaps a little the worse for wear.

Agreed, agreed, I who am on my way, words bellying out my sails, am also that unthinkable ancestor of whom nothing can be said. But perhaps I shall speak of him some day, and of the impenetrable age when I was he, some day when they fall silent, convinced at last I shall never get born, having failed to be conceived. Yes, perhaps I shall speak of him, for an instant, like the echo that mocks, before being restored to him, the one they could not part me from. And indeed they are weakening already, it's perceptible. But it's a feint, to have me rejoice without cause, after their fashion, and accept their terms, for the sake of peace at any price. But I can do nothing, that is what they seem to forget at each instant. I can't rejoice and I can't grieve, it's in vain they explained to me how it's done, I never understood. And what terms? I don't know what it is they want. I say what it is, but I don't know. I emit sounds, better and better it seems to me. If that's not enough for them I can't help it. If I speak of a head, referring to me, it's because I hear it being spoken of. But why keep on saying the same thing? They hope things will change one day, it's natural. That one day on my windpipe, or some other section of the conduit, a nice little abscess will form, with an idea inside, point of departure for a general infection. This would enable me to jubilate like a normal person, knowing why. And in no time I'd be a network of fistulae, bubbling with the blessed pus of reason. Ah if I were flesh and blood, as they are kind enough to posit, I wouldn't say no, there might be something in their little idea. They say I suffer like true thinking flesh, but I'm sorry, I feel nothing. Mahood I felt a little, now and then, but what good did that do them? No, they'd be better advised to try something else. I felt the cang, the flies, the sawdust under my stumps, the tarpaulin on my skull, when they were mentioned to me. But can that be called a life which vanishes when the subject is changed? I don't see why not. But they must have decreed it can't. They are too hard to please, they ask too much. They want me to have a pain in the neck, irrefragable proof of animation, while listening to talk of the heavens. They want me to have a mind where it is known once and for all that I have a pain in the neck, that flies are devouring me and that the heavens can do nothing to help. Let them scourge me without ceasing and evermore, more and more lustily (in view of the habituation factor), in the end I might begin to look as if I had grasped the meaning of life. They might even take a breather from time to time, without my ceasing to howl. For they would have warned me, before they started, You must howl, do you hear, otherwise it proves nothing. And worn out at last, or feeble with old age, and my cries having ceased for want of nourishment, they could pronounce me dead with every appearance of veracity. And without ever having had to move I would have gained my rest and heard them say, striking softly together their dry old hands as if to shake off the dust, He'll never move again. No, that would be too simple. We must have the heavens and God knows what besides, lights, luminaries, the three-monthly ray of hope and the gleam of consolation. But let us close this parenthesis and, with a light heart, open the next. The noise. How long did I remain a pure ear? Up to the moment when it could go on no longer, being too good to last, compared to what was coming. These millions of different sounds, always the same, recurring without pause, are all one requires to sprout a head, a bud to begin with, finally huge, its function first to silence, then to extinguish when the eye joins in, and worse than the evil, its treasure-house. But no lingering on this thin ice. The mechanism matters little, provided I succeed in saying, before I go deaf, It's a voice, and it speaks to me. In inquiring, boldly, if it is not mine. In deciding, it doesn't matter how, that I have none. In blowing darkly hot and cold, with concomitant identical sensations. It's a starting-point, he's off, they don't see me, but they hear me, panting, riveted, they don't know I'm riveted. He knows they are words, he is not sure they are not his, that's how it begins, with such a start no one ever looked back, one day he'll make them his, when he thinks he is alone, far from all men, out of range of every voice, and come to the light of day they keep telling him of. Yes, I know they are words, there was a time I didn't, as I still don't know if they are mine. Their hopes are therefore founded. In their shoes I'd be content with my knowing what I know, I'd demand no more of me than to know that what I hear is not the innocent and necessary sound of dumb things constrained to endure, but the terror-stricken babble of the condemned to silence. I would have pity, give me quittance, not harry me into appearing my own destroyer. But they are severe, greedy, no less, perhaps more, than when I was playing Mahood. Instead of drawing in their horns! It's true I have not spoken yet. In at one ear and incontinent out through the mouth, or the other ear, that's possible too. No sense in multiplying the occasions of error. Two holes and me in the middle, slightly choked. Or a single one, entrance and exit, where the words swarm and jostle like ants, hasty, indifferent, bringing nothing, taking nothing away, too light to leave a mark. I shall not say I again, ever again, it's too farcical. I shall put in its place, whenever I hear it, the third person, if I think of it. Anything to please them. It will make no difference. Where I am there is no one but me, who am not. So much for that. Words, he says he knows they are words. But how can he know, who has never heard anything else? True. Not to mention other things, many others, to which the abundance of matter has unfortunately up to now prohibited the least allusion. For example, to begin with, his breathing. There he is now with breath in his nostrils, it only remains for him to suffocate. The thorax rises and falls, the wear and tear are in full spring, the rot spreads downwards, soon he'll have legs, the possibility of crawling. More lies, he doesn't breathe yet, he'll never breathe. Then what is this faint noise, as of air stealthily stirred, recalling the breath of life, to those whom it corrodes? It's a bad example. But these lights that go out hissing? Is it not more likely a great crackle of laughter, at the sight of his terror and distress? To see him flooded with light, then suddenly plunged back in darkness, must strike them as irresistibly funny. But they have been there so long now, on every side, they may have made a hole in the wall, a little hole, to glue their eyes to, turn about. And these lights are perhaps those they shine upon him, from time to time, in order to observe the progress he is making. But this question of lights deserves to be treated in a section apart, it is so intriguing, and at length, composedly, and so it will be, at the first opportunity, when time is not so short, and the mind more composed. Resolution number twenty-three. And in the meantime the conclusion to be drawn? That the only noises Worm has had till now are those of mouths? Correct. Not forgetting the groaning of the air beneath the burden. He's coming, that's the main thing. When on earth later on the storms rage, drowning momentarily the free expression of opinion, he'll know what is afoot, that the end of the world is not at hand. No, in the place where he is he cannot learn, the head cannot work, he knows no more than on the first day, he merely hears, and suffers, uncomprehending, that must be possible. A head has grown out of his ear, the better to enrage him, that must be it. The head is there, glued to the ear, and in it nothing but rage, that's all that matters, for the time being. It's a transformer in which sound is turned, without the help of reason, to rage and terror, that's all that is required, for the moment. The circumvolutionisation will be seen too later, when they get him out. Why then the human voice, rather than a hyena's howls or the clanging of a hammer? Answer, so that the shock may not be too great, when the writhings of true lips meet his gaze. Between them they find a rejoinder to everything. And how they enjoy talking, they know there is no worse torment, for one not in the conversation. They are numerous, all round, holding hands perhaps, an endless chain, taking turns to talk. They wheel, in jerks, so that the voice always comes from the same quarter. But often they all speak at once, they all say simultaneously the same thing exactly, but so perfectly together that one would take it for a single voice, a single mouth, if one did not know that God alone can fill the rose of the winds, without moving from his place. One, but not Worm, who says nothing, knows nothing, yet. Similarly turn about they benefit by the peephole, those who care to. While one speaks another peeps, the one no doubt whose voice is next due and whose remarks may possibly have reference to what he may possibly have seen, this depending on whether what he has seen has aroused his interest to the extent of appearing worthy of remark, even indirectly. But what hope has sustained them, all the time they have been thus employed? For it is difficult not to suppose them sustained by some form of hope. And what is the nature of the change they are on the look out for, gluing one eye to the hole and closing the other. They have no pedagogic purpose in view, that's definite. There is no question of imparting to him any instruction whatsoever, for the moment. This catechist's tongue, honeyed and perfidious, is the only one they know. Let him move, try and move, that's all they ask, for the moment. No matter where he goes, being at the centre, he will go towards them. So he is at the centre, there is a clue of the highest interest, it matters little to what. They look, to see if he has stirred. He is nothing but a shapeless heap, without a face capable of reflecting the niceties of a torment, but the disposition of which, its greater or lesser degree of crouch and huddledness, is no doubt expressive, for specialists, and enables them to assess the chances of its suddenly making a bound, or dragging its coils faintly away, as if stricken to death. Somewhere in the heap an eye, a wild equine eye, always open, they must have an eye, they see him possessed of an eye. No matter where he goes he will go towards them, towards their song of triumph, when they know he has moved, or towards their sudden silence, when they know he has moved, to make him think he did well to move, or towards the voice growing softer, as if receding, to make him think he is drawing away from them, but not yet far enough, whereas he is drawing nearer, nearer and nearer. No, he can't think anything, can't judge of anything, but the kind of flesh he has is good enough, will try and go where peace seems to be, drop and lie when it suffers no more, or less, or can go no further. Then the voice will begin again, low at first, then louder, coming from the quarter they want him to retreat from, to make him think he is pursued and struggle on, towards them. In this way they'll bring him to the wall, and even to the precise point where they have made other holes through which to pass their arms and seize him. How physical this all is! And then, unable to go any further, because of the obstacle, and unable to go any further in any case, and not needing to go any further for the moment, because of the great silence which has fallen, he will drop, assuming he had risen, but even a reptile can drop, after a long flight, the expression may be used without impropriety. He will drop, it will be his first corner, his first experience of the vertical support, the vertical shelter, reinforcing those of the ground. That must be something, while waiting for oblivion, to feel a prop and buckler, not only for one of one's six planes, but for two, for the first time. But Worm will never know this joy but darkly, being less than a beast, before he is restored, more or less, to that state in which he was before the beginning of his prehistory. Then they will lay hold of him and gather him into their midst. For if they could make a small hole for the eye, then bigger ones for the arms, they can make one bigger still for the transit of Worm, from darkness to light. But what is the good of talking about what they will do as soon as Worm sets himself in motion, so as to gather him without fail into their midst, since he cannot set himself in motion, though he often desires to, if when speaking of him one may speak of desire, and one may not, one should not, but there it is, that is the way to speak of him, that is the way to speak to him, as if he were alive, as if he could understand, as if he could desire, even if it serves no purpose, and it serves none. And it is a blessing for him he cannot stir, even though he suffers because of it, for it would be to sign his life-warrant, to stir from where he is, in search of a little calm and something of the silence of old. But perhaps one day he will stir, the day when the little effort of the early stages, infinitely weak, will have become, by dint of repetition, a great effort, strong enough to tear him from where he lies. Or perhaps one day they will leave him in peace, letting go their hands, filling up the holes and departing, towards more profitable occupations, in Indian file. For a decision must be reached, the scales must tilt, to one side or the other. No, one can spend one's life thus, unable to live, unable to bring to life, and die in vain, having done nothing, been nothing. It is strange they do not go and fetch him in his den, since they seem to have access to it. They dare not, the air in the midst of which he lies is not for them, and yet they want him to breathe theirs. They could set a dog on him perhaps, with instructions to drag him out. But no dog would survive there either, not for one second. With a long pole perhaps, with a hook at the end. But the place where he lies is vast, that's interesting, he is far, too far for them to reach him even with the longest pole. That tiny blur, in the depths of the pit, is he. There he is now in a pit, no avenue will have been left unexplored. They say they see him, the blur is what they see, they say the blur is he, perhaps it is. They say he hears them, they don't know, perhaps he does, yes, he hears, nothing else is certain. Worm hears, though hear is not the word, but it will do, it will have to do. They look down upon him then, according to the latest news, he'll have to climb to reach them. Bah, the latest news, the latest news is not the last. The slopes are gentle that meet where he lies, they flatten out under him, it is not a meeting, it is not a pit, that didn't take long, soon we'll have him perched on an eminence. They don't know what to say, to be able to believe in him, what to invent, to be reassured, they see nothing, they see grey, like still smoke, unbroken, where he might be, if he must be somewhere, where they have decreed he is, into which they launch their voices, one after another, in the hope of dislodging him, hearing him stir, seeing him loom within reach of their gaffs, hooks, barbs, grapnels, saved at last, home at last. And now that's enough about them, their usefulness is over, no, not yet, let them stay, they may still serve, stay where they are, turning in a ring, launching their voices, through the hole, there must be a hole for the voices too. But is it them he hears? Are they really necessary that he may hear, they and kindred puppets? Enough concessions, to the spirit of geometry. He hears, that's all about it, he who is alone, and mute, lost in the smoke, it is not real smoke, there is no fire, no matter, strange hell that has no heating, no denizens, perhaps it's paradise, perhaps it's the light of paradise, and the solitude, and this voice the voice of the blest interceding invisible, for the living, for the dead, all is possible. It isn't the earth, that's all that counts, it can't be the earth, it can't be a hole in the earth, inhabited by Worm alone, or by others if you like, huddled in a heap like him, mute, immovable, and this voice the voice of those who mourn them, envy them, call on them and forget them, that would account for its incoherence, all is possible. Yes, so much the worse, he knows it is a voice, how is not known, nothing is known, he understands nothing it says, just a little, almost nothing, it's inexplicable, but it's necessary, it's preferable, that he should understand just a little, almost nothing, like a dog that always gets the same filth flung to it, the same orders, the same threats, the same cajoleries. That settles that, the end is in sight. But the eye, let's leave him his eye too, it's to see with, this great wild black and white eye, moist, it's to weep with, it's to practise with, before he goes to Killarney. What does he do with it, he does nothing with it, the eye stays open, it's an eye without lids, no need for lids here, where nothing happens, or so little, if he could blink he might miss the odd sight, if he could close it, the kind he is, he'd never open it again. Tears gush from it practically without ceasing, why is not known, nothing is known, whether it's with rage, or whether it's with grief, the fact is there, perhaps it's the voice that makes it weep, with rage, or some other passion, or at having to see, from time to time, some sight or other, perhaps that's it, perhaps he weeps in order not to see, though it seems difficult to credit him with an initiative of this complexity. The rascal, he's getting humanised, he's going to lose if he doesn't watch out, if he doesn't take care, and with what could he take care, with what could he form the faintest conception of the condition they are decoying him into, with their ears, their eyes, their tears and a brainpan where anything may happen. That's his strength, his only strength, that he understands nothing, can't take thought, doesn't know what they want, doesn't know they are there, feels nothing, ah but just a moment, he feels, he suffers, the noise makes him suffer, and he knows, he knows it's a voice, and he understands, a few expressions here and there, a few intonations, ah it looks bad, bad, no, perhaps not, for it's they describe him thus, without knowing, thus because they need him thus, perhaps he hears nothing, suffers nothing, and this eye, more mere imagination. He hears, true, though it's they again who say it, but this can't be denied, this is better not denied. Worm hears, that's all can be said for certain, whereas there was a time he didn't, the same Worm, according to them, he has therefore changed, that's grave, gravid, who knows to what lengths he may be carried, no, he can be relied on. The eye too, of course, is there to put him to flight, make him take fright, badly enough to break his bonds, they call that bonds, they want to deliver him, ah mother of God, the things one has to listen to, perhaps it's tears of mirth. Well, no matter, let's drive on now to the end of the joke, we must be nearly there, and see what they have to offer him, in the way of bugaboos. Who, we? Don't all speak at once, there's no sense in that either. All will come right, later on in the evening, everyone gone and silence restored. In the meantime no sense in bickering about pronouns and other parts of blather. The subject doesn't matter, there is none. Worm being in the singular, as it turned out, they are in the plural, to avoid confusion, confusion is better avoided, pending the great confounding. Perhaps there is only one of them, one would do the trick just as well, but he might get mixed up with his victim, that would be abominable, downright masturbation. We're getting on. Nothing much then in the way of sights for sore eyes. But who can be sure who has not been there, has not lived there, they call that living, for them the spark is present, ready to burst into flame, all it needs is preaching on, to become a living torch, screams included. Then they may go silent, without having to fear an embarrassing silence, when steps are heard on graves as the saying is, genuine hell. Decidedly this eye is hard of hearing. Noises travel, traverse walls, but may the same be said of appearances? By no means, generally speaking. But the present case is rather special. But what appearances, it is always well to try and find out what one is talking about, even at the risk of being deceived. This grey to begin with, meant to be depressing no doubt. And yet there is yellow in it, pink too apparently, it's a nice grey, of the kind recommended as going with everything, urinous and warm. In it the eye can see, otherwise why the eye, but dimly, that's right, no superfluous particulars, later to be controverted. A man would wonder where his kingdom ended, his eye strive to penetrate the gloom, and he crave for a stick, an arm, fingers apt to grasp and then release, at the right moment, a stone, stones, or for the power to utter a cry and wait, counting the seconds, for it to come back to him, and suffer, certainly, at having neither voice nor other missile, nor limbs submissive to him, bending and unbending at the word of command, and perhaps even regret being a man, under such conditions, that is to say a head abandoned to its ancient solitary resources. But Worm suffers only from the noise which prevents him from being what he was before, admire the nuance. If it's the same Worm, and they have set their hearts on it. And if it is not it makes no difference, he suffers as he has always suffered, from this noise that prevents nothing, that must be feasible. In any case this grey can hardly be said to add to his misery, brightness would be better suited for that purpose, since he cannot close his eye. He cannot avert it either, nor lower it, nor lift it up, it remains trained on the same tiny field, a stranger forever to the boons and blessings of accommodation.

But perhaps one day brightness will come, little by little, or rapidly, or in a sudden flood, and then it is hard to see how Worm could stay, and it is also hard to see how he could go. But impossible situations cannot be prolonged, unduly, the fact is well known, either they disperse, or else they turn out to be possible after all, it's only to be expected, not to mention other possibilities. Let there then be light, it will not necessarily be disastrous. Or let there be none, we'll manage without it. But these lights, in the plural, which rear aloft, swell, sweep down and go out hissing, reminding one of the naja, perhaps the moment has come to throw them into the balance and have done with this tedious equipoise, at last. No, the moment has not yet come, to do that. Ha. None of your hoping here, that would spoil everything. Let others hope for him, outside, in the cool, in the light, if they have a wish to, or if they are obliged to, or if they are paid to, yes, they must be paid to hope, they hope nothing, they hope things will continue as they are, it's a soft job, their thoughts wander as they call on Jude, it's praying they are, praying for Worm, praying to Worm, to have pity, pity on them, pity on Worm, they call that pity, merciful God, the things one has to put up with, fortunately it all means nothing to him. Currish obscurity, to thy kennel, hell-hound! Grey. What else? Calm, calm, there must be something else, to go with this grey, which goes with everything.

There must be something of everything here, as in every world, a little of everything. Mighty little, it seems. Beside the point in any case. What balls is going on before this impotent crystalline, that's all that needs to be imagined. A face, how encouraging that would be, if it could be a face, every now and then, always the same, methodically varying its expressions, doggedly demonstrating all a true face can do, without ever ceasing to be recognisable as such, passing from unmixed joy to the sullen fixity of marble, via the most characteristic shades of disenchantment, how pleasant that would be. Worth ten of Saint Anthony's pig's arse. Passing by at the right distance, the right level, say once a month, that's not exorbitant, full face and profile, like criminals. It might even pause, open its mouth, raise its eyebrows, bless its soul, stutter, mutter, howl, groan and finally shut up, the chaps clenched to crack-ing point, or fallen, to let the dribble out. That would be nice. A presence at last. A visitor, faithful, with his visiting-day, his visiting-hour, never staying too long, it would be wearisome, or too little, it would not be enough, but just the necessary time for hope to be born, grow, languish and die, say five minutes. And even should the notion of time dawn on his darkness, at this punctual image of the countenance everlasting, who could blame him? Involving very naturally that of space, they have taken to going hand in hand, in certain quarters, it's safer. And the game would be won, lost and won, he'd be somehow suddenly among us, among the rendezvous, and people saying, Look at old Worm, waiting for his sweetheart, and the flowers, look at the flowers, you'd think he was asleep, you know old Worm, waiting for his love, and the daisies, look at the daisies, you'd think he was dead. That would be worth seeing. Fortunately it's all a dream. For here there is no face, nor anything resembling one, nothing to reflect the joy of living and succedanea, nothing for it but to try something else. Some simple thing, a box, a piece of wood, to come to rest before him for an instant, once a year, once every two years, a ball, revolving one knows not how about one knows not what, about him, every two years, every three years, frequency unimportant in the early stages, without stopping, it needn't stop, that would be better than nothing, he'd hear it approaching, hear it receding, it would be an event, he might learn to count, the minutes, the hours, to fret, be brave, have patience, lose patience, turn his head, roll his eye, a big stone, and faithful, that would be better than nothing, pending the hearts of flesh. And even should his start off, his heart that is, on its waltz, in his ear, tralatralay pom pom, again, tralatralay pom pom, re mi re do bang bang, who could reprehend him? Unfortunately we must stick to the facts, for what else is there, to stick to, to cling to, when all founders, but the facts, when there are any, still floating, within reach of the heart, happy expression that, of the heart crying out, The facts are there, the facts are there, and then more calmly, when the danger is past, the continuation, namely, in the case before us, Here there is no wood, nor any stone, or if there is, the facts are there, it's as if there wasn't, the facts are there, no vegetables, no minerals, only Worm, kingdom unknown, Worm is there, as it were, as it were. But not too fast, it's too soon, to return, to where I am, empty-handed, in triumph, to where I'm waiting, calm, passably calm, knowing, thinking I know, that nothing has befallen me, nothing will befall me, nothing good, nothing bad, nothing to be the death of me, nothing to be the life of me, it would be premature. I see me, I see my place, there is nothing to show it, nothing to distinguish it, from all the other places, they are mine, all mine, if I wish, I wish none but mine, there is nothing to mark it, I am there so little, I see it, I feel it round me, it enfolds me, it covers me, if only this voice would stop, for a second, it would seem long to me, a second of silence. I'd listen, I'd know if it was going to start again, or if it was stilled for ever, what would I know it with, I'd know. And I'd keep on listening, to try and advance in their good graces, keep my place in their favour, and be ready, in case they judged fit to take me in hand again, or I'd stop, stop listening, is it possible that one day I shall stop listening, without having to fear the worst, namely, I don't know, what can be worse than this, a woman's voice perhaps, I hadn't thought of that, they might engage a soprano. But let us leave these dreams and try again. If only I knew what they want, they want me to be Worm, but I was, I was, what's wrong, I was, but ill, it must be that, it can only be that, what else can it be, but that, I didn't report in the light, the light of day, in their midst, to hear them say, Didn't we tell you you were alive and kicking? I have endured, that must be it, I shouldn't have endured, but I feel nothing, yes, yes, this voice, I have endured it, I didn't fly from it, I should have fled, Worm should have fled, but where, how, he's riveted, Worm should have dragged himself away, no matter where, towards them, towards the azure, but how could he, he can't stir, it needn't be bonds, there are no bonds here, it's as if he were rooted, that's bonds if you like, the earth would have to quake, it isn't earth, one doesn't know what it is, it's like sargasso, no, it's like molasses, no, no matter, an eruption is what's needed, to spew him into the light. But what calm, apart from the discourse, not a breath, it's suspicious, the calm that precedes life, no no, not all this time, it's like slime, paradise, it would be paradise, but for this noise, it's life trying to get in, no, trying to get him out, or little bubbles bursting all around, no, there's no air here, air is to make you choke, light is to close your eyes, that's where he must go, where it's never dark, but here it's never dark either, yes, here it's dark, it's they who make this grey, with their lamps. When they go, when they go silent, it will be dark, not a sound, not a glimmer, but they'll never go, yes, they'll go, they'll go silent perhaps and go, one day, one evening, slowly, sadly, in Indian file, casting long shadows, towards their master, who will punish them, or who will spare them, what else is there, up above, for those who lose, punishment, pardon, so they say. What have you done with your material? We have left it behind. But commanded to say whether yes or no they filled up the holes, have you filled up the holes yes or no, they will say yes and no, or some yes, others no, at the same time, not knowing what answer the master wants, to his question. But both are defendable, both yes and no, for they filled up the holes, if you like, and if you don't like they didn't, for they didn't know what to do, on departing, whether to fill up the holes or, on the contrary, leave them gaping wide. So they fixed their lamps in the holes, their long lamps, to prevent them from closing of themselves, it's like potter's clay, their powerful lamps, lit and trained on the within, to make him think they are still there, notwithstanding the silence, or to make him think the grey is natural, or to make him go on suffering, for he does not suffer from the noise alone, he suffers from the grey too, from the light, he must, it's preferable, or to make it possible for them to come back, if the master commands them to, without his knowing they have gone, as if he could know, or for no other reason than their ignorance of what to do, whether to fill up the holes or let them fill up of themselves, it's like shit, there we have it at last, there it is at last, the right word, one has only to seek, seek in vain, to be sure of finding in the end, it's a question of elimination. Enough now about holes. The grey means nothing, the grey silence is not necessarily a mere lull, to be got through somehow, it may be final, or it may not. But the lamps unattended will not burn on forever, on the contrary, they will go out, little by little, without attendants to charge them anew, and go silent, in the end. Then it will be black. But it is with the black as with the grey, the black proves nothing either, as to the nature of the silence which it inspissates (as it were). For they may come back, long after the lights are spent, having pleaded for years in vain before the master and failed to convince him there is nothing to be done, with Worm, for Worm. Then all will start over again, obviously. So it will never be known, Worm will never know, let the silence be black, or let it be grey, it can never be known, as long as it lasts, whether it is final, or whether it is a mere lull, and what a lull, when he must listen, strain his ears for the murmurs of olden silences, hold himself ready for the next instalment, under pain of supplementary thunderbolts. But Worm must not be confused with another. Though this has no importance, as it happens. For he who has once had to listen will listen always, whether he knows he will never hear anything again, or whether he does not. In other words, they like other words, no doubt about it, silence once broken will never again be whole. Is there then no hope? Good gracious, no, heavens, what an idea! Just a faint one perhaps, but which will never serve. But one forgets. And if there is only one he will depart all alone, towards his master, and his long shadow will follow him, across the desert, it's a desert, that's news, Worm will see the light in a desert, the light of day, the desert day, the day they catch him, it's the same as everywhere else, they say not, they say it's purer, clearer, fat lot of difference that will make, oh it is not necessarily the Sahara, or Gobi, there are others, it's the ozone that matters, in the beginning, yes indeed, in the end too, it sterilises. But this livid eye, what use is it to him? To see the light, they call that seeing, no objection, since it causes him suffering, they call that suffering, they know how to cause suffering, the master explained to them, Do this, do that, you'll see him squirm, you'll hear him weep. He weeps, it's a fact, oh not a very firm one, to be made the most of quick. As for the squirming, nothing doing. But there is always this to be said, things are only beginning, though long since begun, they will not lose heart, they'll remember the motto of William the Silent and keep on talking, that's what they're paid for, not for results. Enough about them, they can speak of nothing else, all is theirs, but for them there would be nothing, not even Worm, he's an idea they have, a word they use, when speaking of them, enough about them. But this grey, this light, if he could escape from this light, which makes him suffer, is it not obvious it would make him suffer more and more, in whatever direction he went, since he is at the centre, and drive him back there, after forty or fifty vain excursions? No, that is not obvious. For it is obvious the light would lessen as he went towards it, they would see to that, to make him think he was on the right road and so bring him to the wall. Then the blaze, the capture and the paean. As long as he suffers there's hope, even though they need none, to make him suffer. But how can they know he suffers? Do they see him? They say they do. But it's impossible. Hear him? Certainly not. He makes no noise. A little with his whining perhaps. In any case they are easy, rightly or wrongly, in their minds, he suffers, and thanks to them. Oh not yet sufficiently, but gently does it, an excess of severity at this stage might darken his understanding forever. Another thing. The problem is delicate. The dulling effect of habit, how do they deal with that? They can combat it of course, raising the voice, increasing the light. But suppose, instead of suffering less, as time flies, he continues to suffer as much, precisely, as the first day. That must be possible. And but suppose, instead of suffering less than the first day, or no less, he suffers more and more, as time flies, and the metamorphosis is accomplished, of unchanging future into unchangeable past. Eh? Another thing, but of a different order. The affair is thorny. Is not a uniform suffering preferable to one which, by its ups and downs, is liable at certain moments to encourage the view that perhaps after all it is not eternal? That must depend on the object pursued. Namely? A little fit of impatience, on the part of the patient. Thank you. That is the immediate object. Afterwards there will be others. Afterwards he'll be given lessons in keeping quiet. But for the moment let him toss and turn at least, roll on the ground, damn it all, since there's no other remedy, anything at all, to relieve the monotony, damn it all, look at the burnt alive, they don't have to be told, when not lashed to the stake, to rush about in every direction, without method, crackling, in search of a little cool, there are even those whose sang-froid is such that they throw themselves out of the window. No one asks him to go to those lengths. But simply to discover, without further assistance from without, the alleviations of flight from self, that's all, he won't go far, he needn't go far. Simply to find within himself a palliative for what he is, through no fault of his own. Simply to imitate the hussar who gets up on a chair the better to adjust the plume of his busby, it's the least he might do. No one asks him to think, simply to suffer, always in the same way, without hope of diminution, without hope of dissolution, it's no more complicated than that. No need to think in order to despair. Agreed then on monotony, it's more stimulating. But how can it be ensured? No matter, no matter how, they are doing the best they can, with the miserable means at their disposal, a voice, a little light, poor devils, that's what they're paid for, they say, No sign of hardening, no sign of softening, impossible to say, no matter, it's a good average, we have only to continue, one day he'll understand, one day he'll thrill, the little spasm will come, a change in the eye, and cast him up among us. To be on the watch and never sight, to listen for the moan that never comes, that's not a life worth living either. And yet it's theirs. He is there, says the master, somewhere, do as I tell you, bring him before me, he's lacking to my glory. But one last effort, one more, that's the spirit, that's the way, each time as if it were the last, the only way not to lose ground. A great gulp of stinking air and off we go, we'll be back in a second. Forward! That's soon said. But where is forward? And why? The dirty pack of fake maniacs, they know I don't know, they know I forget all they say as fast as they say it. These little pauses are a poor trick too. When they go silent, so do I. A second later, I'm a second behind them, I remember a second, for the space of a second, that is to say long enough to blurt it out, as received, while receiving the next, which is none of my business either. Not an instant I can call my own and they want me to know where next to turn. Ah I know what I'd know, and where I'd turn, if I had a head that worked. Let them tell me again what I'm doing, if they want me to look as if I were doing it. This tone, these words, to make me think they come from me. Always the same old dodges, ever since they took it into their heads that my existence is only a question of time. I think I must have blackouts, whole sentences lost, no, not whole. Perhaps I've missed the keyword to the whole business. I wouldn't have understood it, but I would have said it, that's all that's required, it would have spoken in my favour, next time they judge me, well well, so they judge me from time to time, they neglect nothing. Perhaps one day I'll know, say, what I'm guilty of. How many of us are there altogether, finally? And who is holding forth at the moment? And to whom? And about what? These are futile teasers. Let them put into my mouth at last the words that will save me, damn me, and no more talk about it, no more talk about anything. But this is my punishment, my crime is my punishment, that's what they judge me for, I expiate vilely, like a pig, dumb, uncomprehending, possessed of no utterance but theirs. They'll clap me in a dungeon, I'm in a dungeon, I've always been in a dungeon, I hear everything, every word they say, it's the only sound, as if I were speaking, to myself, out loud, in the end you don't know any more, a voice that never stops, where it's coming from. Perhaps there are others here, with me, it's dark, very properly, it is not necessarily an oubliette for one, or one other, perhaps I have a companion in misfortune, given to talking, or condemned to talk, you know, any old thing, out loud, without ceasing, but I think not, what do I think not, that I have a companion in misfortune, that's it, that would surprise me, they loathe me, but not to that extent, they say that would surprise me. I must doze off from time to time, with open eyes, and yet nothing changes, ever. Gaps, there have always been gaps, it's the voice stopping, it's the voice failing to carry to me, what can it matter, perhaps it's important, the result is the same, one perhaps that doesn't count, exceptionally. They shut me up here, now they're trying to get me out, to shut me up somewhere else, or to let me go, they are capable of putting me out just to see what I'd do. Standing with their backs to the door, their arms folded, their legs crossed, they would observe me. Or all they did was to find me here, on their arrival, or long afterwards. They are not interested in me, only in the place, they want the place for one of their own. What can one do but speculate, speculate, until one hits on the happy speculation? When all goes silent, and comes to an end, it will be because the words have been said, those it behoved to say, no need to know which, no means of knowing which, they'll be there somewhere, in the heap, in the torrent, not necessarily the last, they have to be ratified by the proper authority, that takes time, he's far from here, they bring him the verbatim report of the proceedings, once in a way, he knows the words that count, it's he who chose them, in the meantime the voice continues, while the messenger goes towards the master, and while the master examines the report, and while the messenger comes back with the verdict, the words continue, the wrong words, until the order arrives, to stop everything or to continue everything, no, superfluous, everything will continue automatically, until the order arrives, to stop everything. Perhaps they are somewhere there, the words that count, in what has just been said, the words it behoved to say, they need not be more than a few. They say they, speaking of them, to make me think it is I who am speaking. Or I say they, speaking of God knows what, to make me think it is not I who am speaking. Or rather there is silence, from the moment the messenger departs until he returns with his orders, namely, Continue. For there are long silences from time to time, truces, and then I hear them whispering, some perhaps whispering, It's over, this time we've hit the mark, and others, We'll have to go through it all again, in other words, or in the same words, arranged differently. Respite then, once in a way, if one can call that respite, when one waits to know one's fate, saying, Perhaps it's not that at all, and saying, Where do these words come from that pour out of my mouth, and what do they mean, no, saying nothing, for the words don't carry any more, if one can call that waiting, when there's no reason for it, and one listens, that stet, without reason, as one has always listened, because one day listening began, because it cannot stop, that's not a reason, if one can call that respite. But what's all this about not being able to die, live, be born, that must have some bearing, all this about staying where you are, dying, living, being born, unable to go forward or back, not knowing where you came from, or where you are, or where you're going, or that it's possible to be elsewhere, to be otherwise, supposing nothing, asking yourself nothing, you can't, you're there, you don't know who, you don't know where, the thing stays where it is, nothing changes, within it, outside it, apparently, apparently. And there is nothing for it but to wait for the end, nothing but for the end to come, and at the end all will be the same, at the end at last perhaps all the same as before, as all that livelong time when there was nothing for it but to get to the end, or fly from it, or wait for it, trembling or not, resigned or not, the nuisance of doing over, and of being, same thing, for one who could never do, never be. Ah if only this voice could stop, this meaningless voice which prevents you from being nothing, just barely prevents you from being nothing and nowhere, just enough to keep alight this little yellow flame feebly darting from side to side, panting, as if straining to tear itself from its wick, it should never have been lit, or it should never have been fed, or it should have been put out, put out, it should have been let go out. Regretting, that's what helps you on, that's what gets you on towards the end of the world, regretting what is, regretting what was, it's not the same thing, yes, it's the same, you don't know, what's happening, what's happened, perhaps it's the same, the same regrets, that's what transports you, towards the end of regretting. But a little animation now for pity's sake, it's now or never, a little spirit, it won't produce anything, not a budge, that doesn't matter, we are not tradesmen, and one never knows, does one, no. Perhaps Mahood will emerge from his urn and make his way towards Montmartre, on his belly, singing, I come, I come, my heart's delight. Or Worm, good old Worm, perhaps he won't be able to bear any more, of not being able, of not being able to bear any more, it would be a pity to miss that. If I were they I'd set the rats on him, water-rats, sewer-rats, they're the best, oh not too many, a dozen to a dozen and a half, that might help him make up his mind, to get going, and what an introduction, to his future attributes. No, it would be in vain, a rat wouldn't survive there, not one second. But let's have another squint at his eye, that's the place to look. A little raw perhaps, the white, with all the pissing, there's a gleam at last, one hesitates to say of intelligence. Apart from that the same as ever. A trifle more prominent perhaps, more paraphimotically globose. It seems to listen. It's weakening, that's unavoidable, glazing, it's high time to offer it something to bring it clean out of its socket, in ten years it will be too late. The mistake they make of course is to speak of him as if he really existed, in a specific place, whereas the whole thing is no more than a project for the moment. But let them blunder on to the end of their folly, then they can go into the question again, taking care not to compromise themselves by the use of terms, if not of notions, accessible to the understanding. In the same way the case of Mahood has been insufficiently studied. One may experience the need of such creatures, assuming they are twain, and even the presentiment of their possible reality, without all these blind and surly disquisitions. A little more reflection would have shown them that the hour to speak, far from having struck, might never strike. But they are compelled to speak, it is forbidden them to stop. Why then not speak of something else, something the existence of which seems in a certain measure already established, on the subject of which one may chatter away without blushing purple every thirty or forty thousand words at having to employ such locutions and which moreover, supreme guarantee, has caused the glibbest tongues to wag from time immemorial, it would be preferable. It's the old story, they want to be entertained, while doing their dirty work, no, not entertained, soothed, no, that's not it either, solaced, no, even less, no matter, with the result they achieve nothing, neither what they want, without knowing exactly what, nor the obscure infamy to which they are committed, the old story. You wouldn't think it was the same gang as a moment ago, or would you? What can you expect, they don't know who they are either, nor where they are, nor what they're doing, nor why everything is going so badly, so abominably badly, that must be it. So they build up hypotheses that collapse on top of one another, it's human, a lobster couldn't do it. Ah a nice mess we're in, the whole pack of us, is it possible we're all in the same boat, no, we're in a nice mess each one in his own peculiar way. I myself have been scandalously bungled, they must be beginning to realise it, I on whom all dangles, better still, about whom, much better, all turns, dizzily, yes yes, don't protest, all spins, it's a head, I'm in a head, what an illumination, sssst, pissed on out of hand. Ah this blind voice, and these moments of held breath when all listen wildly, and the voice that begins to fumble again, without knowing what it's looking for, and again the tiny silence, and the listening again, for what, no one knows, a sign of life perhaps, that must be it, a sign of life escaping someone, and bound to be denied if it came, that's it surely, if only all that could stop, there'd be peace, no, too good to be believed, the listening would go on, for the voice to begin again, for a sign of life, for someone to betray himself, or for something else, anything, what else can there be but signs of life, the fall of a pin, the stirring of a leaf, or the little cry that frogs give when the scythe slices them in half, or when they are spiked, in their pools, with a spear, one could multiply the examples, it would even be an excellent idea, but there it is, one can't. Perhaps it would be better to be blind, the blind hear better, full of general knowledge we are this evening, we have even piano-tuners up our sleeve, they strike A and hear G, two minutes later, there's nothing to be seen in any case, this eye is an oversight. But this isn't Worm speaking. True, so far, who denies it, it would be premature. Nor I, for that matter, and Mahood is notoriously aphonic. But the question is not there, for the moment, no one knows where it is, but it is not there, for the time being. Ah yes, there's great fun to be had from an

139

eye, it weeps for the least little thing, a yes, a no, the yesses make it weep, the noes too, the perhapses particularly, with the result that the grounds for these staggering pronouncements do not always receive the attention they deserve. Mahood too, I mean Worm, no, Mahood, Mahood too is a great weeper, in case it hasn't been mentioned, his beard is soaking with the muck, it's quite ridiculous, especially as it doesn't relieve him in the slightest, what could it possibly relieve him of, the poor brute is as cold as a fish, incapable even of cursing his creator, it's purely mechanical. But it's time Mahood was forgotten, he should never have been mentioned. No doubt. But is it possible to forget him? It is true one forgets everything. And yet it is greatly to be feared that Mahood will never let himself be completely resorbed. Worm yes, Worm will vanish utterly, as if he had never been, which indeed is probably the case, as if one could ever vanish utterly without having been at some previous stage. That's soon said. But Mahood too for that matter. It's not clear, tut tut, it's not clear at all. No matter, Mahood will stay where he was put, stuck up to his skull in his vase, opposite the shambles, beseeching the passers-by, without a word, or a gesture, or any play of his features, they don't play, to perceive him ostensibly, concomitantly with the day's dish, or independently, for reasons unknown, perhaps in the hope of being proven in the swim, that is to say guaranteed to sink, sooner or later, that must be it, such notions may be entertained, without any process of thought. I myself am exceptionally given to the tear, I should have preferred this kept dark, in their position I should have omitted this detail, the truth being I have no vent at my disposal, neither the afore-said nor those less noble, how can one enjoy good health under such conditions, and what is one to believe, that is not the point, to believe this or that, the point is to guess right, nothing more, they say, If it's not white it's very likely black, it must be admitted the method lacks subtlety, in view of the intermediate shades all equally worthy of a chance. The time they waste repeating the same thing, when they must know pertinently it is not the right one. Recriminations easily rebutted, if they chose to take the trouble, and had the leisure, to reflect on their inanity. But how can you think and speak at the same time, how can you think about what you have said, may say, are saying, and at the same time go on with the last-mentioned, you think about any old thing, you say any old thing, more or less, more or less, in a daze of baseless unanswerable self-reproach, that's why they always repeat the same thing, the same old litany, the one they know by heart, to try and think of something different, of how to say something different from the same old thing, always the same wrong thing said always wrong, they can find nothing, nothing else to say but the thing that prevents them from finding, they'd do better to think of what they're saying, in order at least to vary its presentation, that's what matters, but how can you think and speak at the same time, without a special gift, your thoughts wander, your words too, far apart, no, that's an exaggeration, apart, between them would be the place to be, where you suffer, rejoice, at being bereft of speech, bereft of thought, and feel nothing, hear nothing, know nothing, say nothing, are nothing, that would be a blessed place to be, where you are. It's a lucky thing they are there, meaning anywhere, to bear the responsibility of this state of affairs, with respect to which if one does not know a great deal one knows at least this, that one would not care to have it on one's conscience, to have it on one's stomach is enough. Yes, I'm a lucky man to have them, these voluble shades, I'll be sorry when they go, for I won't have them always, not at this rate, they'll make me believe I've piped up before they're done with me. The master in any case, we don't intend, listen to them hedging, we don't intend, unless absolutely driven to it, to make the mistake of inquiring into him, he'd turn out to be a mere high official, we'd end up by needing God, we have lost all sense of decency admittedly, but there are still certain depths we prefer not to sink to. Let us keep to the family circle, it's more intimate, we all know one another now, no surprises to be feared, the will has been opened, nothing for anybody. This eye, curious how this eye invites inspection, demands sympathy, solicits attention, implores assistance, to do what, it's not clear, to stop weeping, have a quick look round, goggle an instant and close forever. It's it you see and it alone, it's from it you set out to look for a face, to it you return having found nothing, nothing worth having, nothing but a kind of ashen smear, perhaps it's long grey hair, hanging in a tangle round the mouth, greasy with ancient tears, or the fringe of a mantle spread like a veil, or fingers opening and closing to try and shut out the world, or all together, fingers, hair and rags, mingled inextricably. Suppositions all equally vain, it's enough to enounce them to regret having spoken, familiar torment, a different past, it's often to be wished, different from yours, when you find out what it was. He is hairless and naked and his hands, laid flat on his knees once and for all, are in no danger of ever getting into mischief. And the face? Balls, all balls, I don't believe in the eye either, there's nothing here, nothing to see, nothing to see with, merciful coincidence, when you think what it would be, a world without spectator, and vice versa, brrr! No spectator then, and better still no spectacle, good riddance. If this noise would stop there'd be nothing more to say. I wonder what the chat is about at the moment. Worm presumably, Mahood being abandoned. And I await my turn. Yes indeed, I do not despair, all things considered, of drawing their attention to my case, some fine day. Not that it offers the least interest, hey, something wrong there, not that it is particularly interesting, I'll accept that, but it's my turn, I too have the right to be shown impossible. This will never end, there's no sense in fooling oneself, yes it will, they'll come round to it, after me it will be the end, they'll give up, saying, It's all a bubble, we've been told a lot of lies, he's been told a lot of lies, who he, the master, by whom, no one knows, the everlasting third party, he's the one to blame, for this state of affairs, the master's not to blame, neither are they, neither am I, least of all I, we were foolish to accuse one another, the master me, them, himself, they me, the master, themselves, I them, the master, myself, we are all innocent, enough. Innocent of what, no one knows, of wanting to know, wanting to be able, of all this noise about nothing, of this long sin against the silence that enfolds us, we won't ask any more, what it covers, this innocence we have fallen to, it covers everything, all faults, all questions, it puts an end to questions. Then it will be over, thanks to me all will be over, and they'll depart, one by one, or they'll drop, they'll let themselves drop, where they stand, and never move again, thanks to me, who could understand nothing, of all they deemed it their duty to tell me, do nothing, of all they deemed it their duty to tell me to do, and upon us all the silence will fall again, and settle, like dust of sand, on the arena, after the massacres. Bewitching prospect if ever there was one, they are beginning to come round to my opinion, after all it's possible I have one, they make me say, If only this, if only that, but the idea is theirs, no, the idea is not theirs either. As far as I personally am concerned there is every likelihood of my being incapable of ever desiring or deploring anything whatsoever. For it would seem difficult for someone, if I may so describe myself, to aspire towards a situation of which, notwithstanding the enthusiastic descriptions lavished on him, he has not the remotest idea, or to desire with a straight face the cessation of that other, equally unintelligible, assigned to him in the beginning and never modified. This silence they are always talking about, from which supposedly he came, to which he will return when his act is over, he doesn't know what it is, nor what he is meant to do, in order to deserve it. That's the bright boy of the class speaking now, he's the one always called to the rescue when things go badly, he talks all the time of merit and situations, he has saved more than one, of suffering too, he knows how to stimulate the flagging spirit, stop the rot, with the simple use of this mighty word alone, even if he has to add, a moment later, But what suffering, since he has always suffered, which rather damps the rejoicings. But he

145

soon makes up for it, he puts all to rights again, invoking the celebrated notions of quantity, habit-formation, wear and tear, and others too numerous for him to mention, and which he is thus in a position, in the next belch, to declare inapplicable to the case before him, for there is no end to his wits. But, see above, have they not already bent over me till black and blue in the face, nay, have they ever done anything else, during the past – no, no dates for pity's sake, and another question, what am I doing in Mahood's story, and in Worm's, or rather what are they doing in mine, there are some irons in the fire to be going on with, let them melt. Oh I know, I know, attention please, this may mean something, I know, there's nothing new there, it's all part of the same old irresistible baloney, namely, But my dear man, come, be reasonable, look, this is you, look at this photograph, and here's your file, no convictions, I assure you, come now, make an effort, at your age, to have no identity, it's a scandal, I assure you, look at this photograph, what, you see nothing, true for you, no matter, here, look at this death's-head, you'll see, you'll be all right, it won't last long, here, look, here's the record, insults to policemen, indecent exposure, sins against holy ghost, contempt of court, impertinence to superiors, impudence to inferiors, deviations from reason, without battery, look, no battery, it's nothing, you'll be all right, you'll see, I beg your pardon, does he work, good God no, out of the question, look, here's the medical report, spasmodic tabes, painless ulcers, I repeat, painless, all is painless, multiple softenings, manifold hardenings, insensitive to blows, sight failing, chronic gripes, light diet, shit well tolerated, hearing failing, heart irregular, sweet-tempered, smell failing, heavy sleeper, no erections, would you like some more, commission in the territorials, inoperable, untransportable, look, here's the face, no no, the other end, I assure you, it's a bargain, I beg your pardon, does he drink, good God yes, passionately, I beg your pardon, father and mother, both dead, at seven months interval, he at the conception, she at the nativity, I assure you, you won't do better, at your age, no human shape, the pity of it, look, here's the photograph, you'll see, you'll be all right, what does it amount to, after all, a painful moment, on the surface, then peace, underneath, it's the only way, believe me, the only way out, I beg your pardon, have I nothing else, why certainly, certainly, just a second, curious you should mention it, I was wondering myself, just a second, if you were not rather, just a second, here we are, this one here, but I wanted to be sure, what, you don't understand, neither do I, no matter, it's no time for levity, yes, I was right, no doubt about it this time, it's you all over, look, here's the photograph, take a look at that, dying on his feet, you'd better hurry, it's a bargain, I assure you, and so on, till

I'm tempted, no, all lies, they know it well, I never understood, I haven't stirred, all I've said, said I've done, said I've been, it's they who said it, I've said nothing, I haven't stirred, they don't understand, I can't stir, they think I don't want to, that their conditions don't suit me, that they'll hit on others, in the end, to my liking, then I'll stir, I'll be in the bag, that's how I see it, I see nothing, they don't understand, I can't go to them, they'll have to come and get me, if they want me, Mahood won't get me out, nor Worm either, they set great store on Worm, to coax me out, he was something new, different from all the others, meant to be, perhaps he was, to me they're all the same, they don't understand, I can't stir, I'm all right here, I'd be all right here, if they'd leave me, let them come and get me, if they want me, they'll find nothing, then they can depart, with an easy mind. And if there is only one, like me, he can depart without fear of remorse, having done all he could, and even more, to achieve the impossible and so lost his life, or stay with me here, he might do that, and be a like for me, that would be lovely, my first like, that would be epoch-making, to know I had a like, a congener, he wouldn't have to be like me, he couldn't but be like me, he need only relax, he might believe what he pleased, at the outset, that he was in hell, or that the place was charming, he might even exclaim, I'll never stir again, being used to announcing his decisions, at the top of his voice, so as to get to know them better, he might even add, to cover all risks, For the moment, it would be his last howler, he need only relax, he'd disappear, he'd know nothing either, there we'd be the two of us, unbeknown to ourselves, unbeknown to each other, that's a darling dream I've been having, a broth of a dream. And it's not over. For here comes another, to see what has happened to his pal, and get him out, and back to his right mind, and back to his kin, with a flow of threats and promises, and tales like this of wombs and cribs, diapers bepissed and the first long trousers, love's young dream and life's old lech, blood and tears and skin and bones and the tossing in the grave, and so coax him out, as he me, that's right, pidgin bullskrit, and in the end, having lived his life, no, before, but you've got my meaning, and there we are the three of us, it's cosier, perpetual dream, you have merely to sleep, not even that, it's like the old jingle. A dog crawled into the kitchen and stole a crust of bread, then cook up with I've forgotten what and walloped him till he was dead, second verse, Then all the dogs came crawling and dug the dog a tomb and wrote upon the tombstone for dogs and bitches to come, third verse, as the first, fourth, as the second, fifth, as the third, give us time, give us time and we'll be a multitude, a thousand, ten thousand, there's no lack of room, adeste, adeste, all ye living bastards, you'll

149

be all right, you'll see, you'll never be born again, what am I saying, you'll never have been born, and bring your brats, our hell will be heaven to them, after what you've done to them. But come to think of it are we not already a goodly company, what right have I to flatter myself I'm the first, first in time I mean of course, there we have a few more questions, please God they don't take the fancy to answer them. What can they be hatching anyhow, at this eleventh hour? Can it be they are resolved at last to seize me by the horns? Looks like it. In that case tableau any minute. Oyez, oyez, I was like them, before being like me, oh the swine, that's one I won't get over in a hurry, no matter, no matter, the charge is sounded, present arms, corpse, to your guns, spermatozoon. I too, weary of pleading an incomprehensible cause, at six and eight the thousand flowers of rhetoric, let myself drop among the contumacious, nice image that, telescoping space, it must be the Pulitzer Prize, they want to bore me to sleep, at long range for fear I might defend myself, they want to catch me alive, so as to be able to kill me, thus I shall have lived, they think I'm alive, what a business, were there but a cadaver it would smack of body-snatching, not in a womb either, the slut has yet to menstruate capable of whelping me, that should singularly narrow the field of research, a sperm dying, of cold, in the sheets, feebly wagging its little tail, perhaps I'm a drying sperm, in the sheets of an innocent boy, even that takes time, no stone must be left unturned, one mustn't be afraid of making a howler, how can one know it is one before it's made, and one it most certainly is, now that it's irrevocable, for the good reason, here's another, here comes another, unless it escapes them in time, what a hope, the bright boy is there, for the excellent reason that counts as living too, counts as murder, it's notorious, ah you can't deny it, some people are lucky, born of a wet dream and dead before morning, I must say I'm tempted, no, the testis has yet to descend that would want any truck with me, it's mutual, another gleam down the drain. And now one last look at Mahood, at Worm, we'll never have another chance, ah will they never learn sense, there's nothing to be got, there was never anything to be got from those stories, I have mine, somewhere, let them tell it to me, they'll see there's nothing to be got from it either, nothing to be got from me, it will be the end, of this hell of stories, you'd think I was cursing them, always the same old trick, you'd be sorry for them, perhaps I'll curse them yet, they'll know what it is to be a subject of conversation, I'll impute words to them you wouldn't throw to a dog, an ear, a mouth and in the middle a few rags of mind, I'll get my own back, a few flitters of mind, they'll see what it's like, I'll clap an eye at random in the thick of the mess, on the off chance something might stray in front of it, then I'll let down my trousers and shit stories on them, stories, photographs, records, sites, lights, gods and fellow-creatures, the daily round and common task, observing the while, Be born, dear friends, be born, enter my arse, you'll just love my colic pains, it won't take long, I've the bloody flux. They'll see what it's like, that it's not so easy as it looks, that you must have a taste for it, that you must be born alive, that it's not something you can acquire, that will teach them perhaps, to keep their nose out of my business. Yes, if I could, but I can't, whatever it is, I can't any more, there was perhaps a time I could, in the days when I was bursting my guts, as per instructions, to bring back to the fold the dear lost lamb, I'd been told he was dear, that he was dear to me, that I was dear to him, that we were dear to each other, all my life I've pelted him with twaddle, the dear departed, wondering what he could possibly be like, wondering where we could possibly have met, all my life, well, almost, damn the almost, all my life, until I joined him, and now it's I am dear to them, now it's they are dear to me, glad to hear it, they'll join us, one by one, what a pity they are numberless, so are we, dear charnel-house of renegades, this evening decidedly everything is dear, no matter, the ancients hear nothing, and my old quarry, there beside me, for him it's all over, beside me how are you, underneath me, we're piled up in heaps, no, that won't work either, no matter, it's a detail, for him it's all over, him the second-last, and for me too, me the last, it will soon be all over, I'll hear nothing more, I've nothing to do, simply wait, it's a slow business, he'll come and lie on top of me, lie beside me, my dear tormentor, his turn to suffer what he made me suffer, mine to be at peace. How all comes right in the end to be sure, it's thanks to patience, thanks to time, it's thanks to the earth that revolves that the earth revolves no more, that time ends its meal and pain comes to an end, you have only to wait, without doing anything, it's no good doing anything, and without understanding, there's no help in understanding, and all comes right, nothing comes right, nothing, nothing, this will never end, this voice will never stop, I'm alone here, the first and the last, I never made anyone suffer, I never stopped anyone's sufferings, no one will ever stop mine, they'll never depart, I'll never stir, I'll never know peace, neither will they, but with this difference, that they don't want it, they say they don't want it, they say I don't want it, don't want peace, after all perhaps they're right, how could I want it, what is it, they say I suffer, perhaps they're right, and that I'd feel better if I did this, said that, if my body stirred, if my head understood, if they went silent and departed, perhaps they're right, how would I know about these things, how would I under-stand what they're talking about. I'll never stir, never speak, they'll never go silent, never depart, they'll never catch me, never stop trying, that's that. I'm listening. Well I prefer that, I must say I prefer that, that what, oh you know, who you, oh I suppose the audience, well well, so there's an audience, it's a public show, you buy your seat and you wait, perhaps it's free, a free show, you take your seat and you wait for it to begin, or perhaps it's compulsory, a compulsory show, you wait for the compulsory show to begin, it takes time, you hear a voice, perhaps it's a recitation, that's the show, someone reciting, selected passages, old favourites, a poetry matinée, or someone improvising, you can barely hear him, that's the show, you can't leave, you're afraid to leave, it might be worse elsewhere, you make the best of it, you try and be reasonable, you came too early, here we'd need Latin, it's only beginning, it hasn't begun, he's only preluding, clearing his throat, alone in his dressing-room, he'll appear any moment, he'll begin any moment, or it's the stage-manager, giving his instructions, his last recommendations, before the curtain rises, that's the show, waiting for the show, to the sound of a murmur, you try and be reasonable, perhaps it's not a voice at all, perhaps it's the air, ascending, descending, flowing, eddying, seeking exit, finding none, and the spectators, where are they, you didn't notice, in the anguish of waiting, never noticed you were waiting alone, that's the show, waiting alone, in the restless air, for it to begin, for something to begin, for there to be something else but you, for the power to rise, the courage to leave, you try and be reasonable, perhaps you are blind, probably deaf, the show is over, all is over, but where then is the hand, the helping hand, or merely charitable, or the hired hand, it's a long time coming, to take yours and draw you away, that's the show, free, gratis and for nothing, waiting alone, blind, deaf, you don't know where, you don't know for what, for a hand to come and draw you away, somewhere else, where perhaps it's worse. And now for the it, I prefer that, I must say I prefer that, what a memory, real flypaper, I don't know, I don't prefer it any more, that's all I know, so why bother about it, a thing you don't prefer, just think of that, bothering about that, perish the thought, one must wait, discover a preference, within one's bosom, then it will be time enough to institute an inquiry. Moreover, that's right, link, link, you never know, moreover their attitude towards me has not changed, I am deceived, they are deceived, they have tried to deceive me, saying their attitude towards me had changed, but they haven't deceived me, I didn't understand what they were trying to do to me, I say what I'm told to say, that's all there is to it, and yet I wonder, I don't know, I don't feel a mouth on me, I don't feel the jostle of words in my mouth, and when you say a poem

you like, if you happen to like poetry, in the under-
ground, or in bed, for yourself, the words are there,
somewhere, without the least sound, I don't feel that
either, words falling, you don't know where, you don't
know whence, drops of silence through the silence, I
don't feel it, I don't feel a mouth on me, nor a head, do
I feel an ear, frankly now, do I feel an ear, well frankly
now I don't, so much the worse, I don't feel an ear
either, this is awful, make an effort, I must feel something, yes, I feel something, they say I feel something,
I don't know what it is, I don't know what I feel, tell me
what I feel and I'll tell you who I am, they'll tell me
who I am, I won't understand, but the thing will be
said, they'll have said who I am, and I'll have heard,
without an ear I'll have heard, and I'll have said it,
without a mouth I'll have said it, I'll have said it inside
me, then in the same breath outside me, perhaps that's
what I feel, an outside and an inside and me in the
middle, perhaps that's what I am, the thing that divides
the world in two, on the one side the outside, on the
other the inside, that can be as thin as foil, I'm neither
one side nor the other, I'm in the middle, I'm the par-
tition, I've two surfaces and no thickness, perhaps
that's what I feel, myself vibrating, I'm the tympanum,
on the one hand the mind, on the other the world, I
don't belong to either, it's not to me they're talking, it's
not of me they're talking, no, that's not it, I feel nothing

of all that, try something else, herd of shites, say something else, for me to hear, I don't know how, for me to say, I don't know how, what clowns they are, to keep on saying the same thing when they know it's not the right one, no, they know nothing either, they forget, they think they change and they never change, they'll be there saying the same thing till they die, then perhaps a little silence, till the next gang arrives on the site, I alone am immortal, what can you expect, I can't get born, perhaps that's their big idea, to keep on saying the same old thing, generation after generation, till I go mad and begin to scream, then they'll say, He's mewled, he'll rattle, it's mathematical, let's get out to hell out of here, no point in waiting for that, others need us, for him it's over, his troubles will be over, he's saved, we've saved him, they're all the same, they all let themselves be saved, they all let themselves be born, he was a tough nut, he'll have a good time, a brilliant career, in fury and remorse, he'll never forgive himself, and so depart, thus communing, in Indian file, or two by two, along the seashore, now it's the seashore, on the shingle, along the sands, in the evening air, it's evening, that's all I know, evening, shadows, somewhere, anywhere, on the earth. Go mad, yes, but there it is, what would I go mad with, and evening isn't sure either, it needn't be evening, dawn too bestows long shadows, on all that is still standing, that's all that matters, only the shadows matter, with no life of their own, no shape and no respite, perhaps it's dawn, evening of night, it doesn't matter, and so depart, towards my brethren, no, none of that, no brethren, that's right, take it back, they don't know, they depart, not knowing whither, towards their master, it's possible, make a note of that, it's just possible, to sue for their freedom, for them it's the end, for me the beginning, my end begins, they stop to listen to my screams, they'll never stop again, yes, they'll stop, my screams will stop, from time to time, I'll stop screaming, to listen and hear if anyone is answering, to look and see if anyone is coming, then go, close my eyes and go, screaming, to scream elsewhere. Yes, my mouth, but there it is, I won't open it, I have no mouth, and what about it, I'll grow one, a little hole at first, then wider and wider, deeper and deeper, the air will gush into me, and out a second later, howling. But is it not rather too much to ask, to ask so much, of so little, is it really politic? And would it not suffice, without any change in the structure of the thing as it now stands, as it always stood, without a mouth being opened at the place which even pain could never line, would it not suffice to, to what, the thread is lost, no matter, here's another, would not a little stir suffice, some tiny subsidence or upheaval, that would start things off, the whole fabric would be infected, the ball would start a-rolling, the disturbance would spread to every part, locomotion itself would soon appear, trips properly so called, business trips, pleasure trips, research expeditions, sabbatical leaves, jaunts and rambles, honeymoons at home and abroad and long sad solitary tramps in the rain, I indicate the main trends, athletics, tossing in bed, physical jerks, locomotor ataxy, death throes, rigor and rigor mortis, emergal of the bony structure, that should suffice. Unfortunately it's a question of words, of voices, one must not forget that, one must try and not forget that completely, of a statement to be made, by them, by me, some slight obscurity here, it might sometimes almost be wondered if all their ballocks about life and death is not as foreign to their nature as it is to mine. The fact is they no longer know where they've got to in their affair, where they've got me to, I never knew, I'm where I always was, wherever that is, and their affair, I don't know what is meant by that, some process no doubt, that I've got stuck in, or haven't yet come to, I've got nowhere, in their affair, that's what galls them, they want me there somewhere, anywhere, if only they'd stop committing reason, on them, on me, on the purpose to be achieved, and simply go on, with no illusion about having begun one day or ever being able to conclude, but it's too difficult, too difficult, for one bereft of purpose, not to look forward to his end, and bereft of all reason to exist, back to a time he did not. Difficult too not to forget, in your thirst for something to do, in order to be done with it, and have that much less to do, that there is nothing to be done, nothing special to be done, nothing doable to be done. No point either, in your thirst, your hunger, no, no need of hunger, thirst is enough, no point in telling yourself stories, to pass the time, stories don't pass the time, nothing passes the time, that doesn't matter, that's how it is, you tell yourself stories, then any old thing, saying, No more stories from this day forth, and the stories go on, it's stories still, or it was never stories, always any old thing, for as long as you can remember, no, longer than that, any old thing, the same old thing, to pass the time, then, as time didn't pass, for no reason at all, in your thirst, trying to cease and never ceasing, seeking the cause, the cause of talking and never ceasing, finding the cause, losing it again, finding it again, not finding it again, seeking no longer, seeking again, finding again, losing again, finding nothing, finding at last, losing again, talking without ceasing, thirstier than ever, seeking as usual, losing as usual, blathering away, wondering what it's all about, seeking what it can be you are seeking, exclaiming, Ah yes, sighing, No no, crying, Enough, ejaculating, Not yet, talking incessantly, any old thing, seeking once more, any old thing, thirsting away, you don't know what for, ah yes, something to do, no no, nothing to be done, and now enough of that, unless perhaps, that's an idea, let's seek over there, one last little effort, seek what, pertinent objection, let us try and determine, before we seek, what it can be, before we seek over there, over where, talking unceasingly, seeking incessantly, in yourself, outside yourself, cursing man, cursing God, stopping cursing, past bearing it, going on bearing it, seeking indefatigably, in the world of nature, the world of man, where is nature, where is man, where are you, what are you seeking, who is seeking, seeking who you are, supreme aberration, where you are, what you're doing, what you've done to them, what they've done to you, prattling along, where are the others, who is talking, not I, where am I, where is the place where I've always been, where are the others, it's they are talking, talking to me, talking of me, I hear them, I'm mute, what do they want, what have I done to them, what have I done to God, what have they done to God, what has God done to us, nothing, and we've done nothing to him, you can't do anything to him, he can't do anything to us, we're innocent, he's innocent, it's nobody's fault, what's nobody's fault, this state of affairs, what state of affairs, so it is, so be it, don't fret, so it will be, how so, rattling on, dying of thirst, seeking determinedly, what they want, they want me to be, this, that, to howl, stir, crawl out of here, be born, die, listen, I'm listening, it's not enough, I must understand, I'm doing my best, I can't understand, I stop doing my best,

161

I can't do my best, I can't go on, poor devil, neither can they, let them say what they want, give me something to do, something doable to do, poor devils, they can't, they don't know, they're like me, more and more, no more need of them, no more need of anyone, no one can do anything, it's I am talking, thirsting, starving, let it stand, in the ice and in the furnace, you feel nothing, strange, you don't feel a mouth on you, you don't feel your mouth any more, no need of a mouth, the words are everywhere, inside me, outside me, well well, a minute ago I had no thickness, I hear them, no need to hear them, no need of a head, impossible to stop them, impossible to stop, I'm in words, made of words, others' words, what others, the place too, the air, the walls, the floor, the ceiling, all words, the whole world is here with me, I'm the air, the walls, the walled-in one, everything yields, opens, ebbs, flows, like flakes, I'm all these flakes, meeting, mingling, falling asunder, wherever I go I find me, leave me, go towards me, come from me, nothing ever but me, a particle of me, retrieved, lost, gone astray, I'm all these words, all these strangers, this dust of words, with no ground for their settling, no sky for their dispersing, coming together to say, fleeing one another to say, that I am they, all of them, those that merge, those that part, those that never meet, and nothing else, yes, something else, that I'm something quite different, a quite different thing, a wordless thing in an empty place, a hard shut dry cold black place, where nothing stirs, nothing speaks, and that I listen, and that I seek, like a caged beast born of caged beasts born of caged beasts born of caged beasts born in a cage and dead in a cage, born and then dead, born in a cage and then dead in a cage, in a word like a beast, in one of their words, like such a beast, and that I seek, like such a beast, with my little strength, such a beast, with nothing of its species left but fear and fury, no, the fury is past, nothing but fear, nothing of all its due but fear centupled, fear of its shadow, no, blind from birth, of sound then, if you like, we'll have that, one must have something, it's a pity, but there it is, fear of sound, fear of sounds, the sounds of beasts, the sounds of men, sounds in the daytime and sounds at night, that's enough, fear of sounds, all sounds, more or less, more or less fear, all sounds, there's only one, continuous, day and night, what is it, it's steps coming and going, it's voices speaking for a moment, it's bodies groping their way, it's the air, it's things, it's the air among the things, that's enough, that I seek, like it, no, not like it, like me, in my own way, what am I saying, after my fashion, that I seek, what do I seek now, what it is, it must be that, it can only be that, what it is, what it can be, what what can be, what I seek, no, what I hear, now it comes back to me, all back to me, they say I seek what it is I hear, I hear them, now it comes back to me, what it can

163

possibly be, and where it can possibly come from, since all is silent here, and the walls thick, and how I manage, without feeling an ear on me, or a head, or a body, or a soul, how I manage, to do what, how I manage, it's not clear, dear dear, you say it's not clear, something is wanting to make it clear, I'll seek, what is wanting, to make everything clear, I'm always seeking something, it's tiring in the end, and it's only the beginning, how I manage, under such conditions, to do what I'm doing, what am I doing, I must find out what I'm doing, tell me what you're doing and I'll ask you how it's possible, I hear, you say I hear, and that I seek, it's a lie, I seek nothing, nothing any more, no matter, let's leave it, no harking, and that I seek, listen to them now, jogging my memory, seek what, firstly what it is, secondly where it comes from, thirdly how I manage, that's it, now we've got it, thirdly how I manage, to do it, seeing that this, considering that that, inasmuch as God knows what, that's clear now, how I manage to hear, and how I manage to understand, it's a lie, what would I understand with, that's what I'm asking, how I manage to understand, oh not the half, nor the hundredth, nor the five thousandth, let us go on dividing by fifty, nor the quarter millionth, that's enough, but a little nevertheless, it's essential, it's preferable, it's a pity, but there it is, just a little all the same, the least possible, it's appreciable, it's enough, the rough meaning of one expression in a thousand, in ten thousand, let us go on multiplying by ten, nothing more restful than arithmetic, in a hundred thousand, in a million, it's too much, too little, we've gone wrong somewhere, no matter, there is no great difference here between one expression and the next, when you've grasped one you've grasped them all, I am not in that fortunate position, all, how you exaggerate, always out for the whole hog, the all of all and the all of nothing, never in the happy golden, never, always, it's too much, too little, often, seldom, let me now sum up, after this digression, there is I, yes, I feel it, I confess, I give in, there is I, it's essential, it's preferable, I wouldn't have said so, I won't always say so, so let me hasten to take advantage of being now obliged to say, in a manner of speaking, that there is I, on the one hand, and this noise on the other, that I never doubted, no, let us be logical, there was never any doubt about that, this noise, on the other, if it is the other, that will very likely be the theme of our next deliberation, I sum up, now that I'm there it's I will do the summing up, it's I will say what is to be said and then say what it was, that will be jolly, I sum up, I and this noise, I see nothing else for the moment, but I have only just taken over my functions, I and this noise, and what about it, don't interrupt me, I'm doing my best, I repeat, I and this noise, on the subject of which, inverting the natural order, we would seem to know for certain, among other things, what follows, namely, on the one hand, with regard to the noise, that it has not been possible up to date to determine with certainty, or even approximately, what it is, in the way of noise, or how it comes to me, or by what organ it is emitted, or by what perceived, or by what intelligence apprehended, in its main drift, and on the other, that is to say with regard to me, this is going to take a little longer, with regard to me, nice time we're going to have now, with regard to me, that it has not yet been our good fortune to establish with any degree of accuracy what I am, where I am, whether I am words among words, or silence in the midst of silence, to recall only two of the hypotheses launched in this connection, though silence to tell the truth does not appear to have been very conspicuous up to now, but appearances may sometimes be deceptive, I resume, not yet our good fortune to establish, among other things, what I am, no, sorry, already mentioned, what I'm doing, how I manage, to hear, if I hear, if it's I who hear, and who can doubt it, I don't know, doubt is present, in this connection, somewhere or other, I resume, how I manage to hear, if it's I who hear, and how to understand, ellipse when possible, it saves time, how to understand, same observation, and how it happens, if it's I who speak, and it may be assumed it is, as it may be suspected it is not, how it happens, if it's I who speak, that I speak without ceasing, that I long to cease, that I can't cease, I indicate the principal divisions, it's more synoptic, I resume, not the good fortune to establish, with regard to me, if it's I who seek, what exactly it is I seek, find, lose, find again, throw away, seek again, find again, throw away again, no, I never threw anything away, never threw anything away of all the things I found, never found anything that I didn't lose, never lost anything that I mightn't as well have thrown away, if it's I who seek, find, lose, find again, lose again, seek in vain, seek no more, if it's I what it is, and if it's not I who it is, and what it is, I see nothing else for the moment, yes I do, I conclude, not the good fortune to establish, considering the futility of my telling myself even any old thing, to pass the time, why I do it, if it's I who do it, as if reasons were required for doing any old thing, to pass the time, no matter, the question may be asked, off the record, why time doesn't pass, doesn't pass, from you, why it piles up all about you, instant on instant, on all sides, deeper and deeper, thicker and thicker, your time, others' time, the time of the ancient dead and the dead yet unborn, why it buries you grain by grain neither dead nor alive, with no memory of anything, no hope of anything, no knowledge of anything, no history and no prospects, buried under the seconds, saying any old thing, your mouth full of sand, oh I know it's imma-terial, time is one thing, I another, but the question may be asked, why time doesn't pass, just like that, off the record, en passant, to pass the time, I think that's all, for the moment, I see nothing else, I see nothing whatever, for the time being. But I really mustn't ask myself any more questions, if it's I, I really must not. More resolutions, while we're at it, that's right, resolutely, more resolutions. Make abundant use of the principle of parsimony, as if it were familiar to me, it is not too late. Assume notably henceforward that the thing said and the thing heard have a common source, resisting for this purpose the temptation to call in question the possibility of assuming anything whatever. Situate this source in me, without specifying where exactly, no finicking, anything is preferable to the consciousness of third parties and, more generally speaking, of an outer world. Carry if necessary this process of compression to the point of abandoning all other postulates than that of a deaf half-wit, hearing nothing of what he says and understanding even less. Evoke at painful junctures, when discouragement threatens to raise its head, the image of a vast cretinous mouth, red, blubber and slobbering, in solitary confinement, extruding indefatigably, with a noise of wet kisses and washing in a tub, the words that obstruct it. Set aside once and for all, at the same time as the analogy with orthodox damnation, all idea of beginning and end. Overcome, that goes without saying, the fatal leaning towards expressiveness. Equate me, without pity or scruple, with him who exists, somehow, no matter how, no finicking, with him whose story this story had the brief ambition to be. Better, ascribe to me a body. Better still, arrogate to me a mind. Speak of a world of my own, sometimes referred to as the inner, without choking. Doubt no more. Seek no more. Take advantage of the brand-new soul and substantiality to abandon, with the only possible abandon, deep down within. And finally, these and other decisions having been taken, carry on cheerfully as before. Something has changed nevertheless. Not a word about Mahood, or Worm, for the past – ah yes, I nearly forgot, speak of time, without flinching, and what is more, it just occurs to me, by a natural association of ideas, treat of space with the same easy grace, as if it were not bunged up on all sides, a few inches away, after all that's something, a few inches, to be thankful for, it gives one air, room for the tongue to loll, to have lolled, to loll on. When I think, that is to say, no, let it stand, when I think of the time I've wasted with these bran-dips, beginning with Murphy, who wasn't even the first, when I had me, on the premises, within easy reach, tottering under my own skin and bones, real ones, rotting with solitude and neglect, till I doubted my own existence, and even still, today, I have no faith in it, none, so that I have to say, when I speak, Who speaks, and seek, and so on and similarly for all the other things that happen to me and for which someone must be found, for things that happen must have someone to happen to, someone must stop them. But Murphy and the others, and last but not least the two old buffers here present, could not stop them, the things that happened to me, nothing could happen to them, of the things that happened to me, and nothing else either, there is nothing else, let us be lucid for once, nothing else but what happens to me, such as speaking, and such as seeking, and which cannot happen to me, which prowl round me, like bodies in torment, the torment of no abode, no repose, no, like hyenas, screeching and laughing, no, no better, no matter, I've shut my doors against them, I'm not at home to anything, my doors are shut against them, perhaps that's how I'll find silence, and peace at last, by opening my doors and letting myself be devoured, they'll stop howling, they'll start eating, the maws now howling. Open up, open up, you'll be all right, you'll see. What a joy it is, to turn and look astern, between two visits to the depths, scan in vain the horizon for a sail, it's a real pleasure, upon my word it is, to be unable to drown, under such conditions. Yes, but there it is, I am far from my doors, far from my walls, someone would have to wake the turnkey, there must be one somewhere, far from my subject too, let us get back to it, it's gone, no longer there where I thought I last saw it, strange this mixture of solid and liquid, where was I, ah yes, my subject, no longer there, or no longer the same, or I mistake the place, no, yes, it's the same, still there, in the same place, it's a pity, I would have liked to lose it, I would have liked to lose me, lose me the way I could long ago, when I still had some imagination, close my eyes and be in a wood, or on the seashore, or in a town where I don't know anyone, it's night, everyone has gone home, I walk the streets, I lash into them one after the other, it's the town of my youth, I'm looking for my mother to kill her, I should have thought of that a bit earlier, before being born, it's raining, I'm all right, I stride along on the crown of the street with great yaws to left and right, now that's all over, with closed eyes I see the same as with them open, namely, wait, I'll say it, I'll try and say it, I'm curious to know what it can possibly be that I see, with closed eyes, with open eyes, nothing, I see nothing, well that is a disappointment, I was hoping for something better than that, is that what it is to be unable to lose yourself, I'm asking myself a question, is that what it is, to see nothing, no matter where I look, nor, eyeless, the little creature in his different guises coming and going, now in shadow, now in light, doing his best, seeking the means of staying among the living, of getting off with his life, or shut up looking out of the window at the ever-changing, is that it, to be unable to lose myself, I don't know, what did I see in the old days, when I ventured a quick look, I don't know, I don't remember. There I am in any case equipped with eyes, which I open and shut, two, perhaps blue, knowing it avails nothing, for I have a head now too, where all manner of things are known, can it be of me I'm speaking, is it possible, of course not, that's another thing I know, I'll speak of me when I speak no more. In any case it's not a question of speaking of me, but of speaking, of speaking no more, this slight confusion augurs well, now I'll have to find a name for this latest surrogate, his head splitting with vile certainties and his doll's eyes, later on, later on, first I must describe him in greater detail, see what he's capable of, whence he comes and whither he returns, in his head of course, we don't intend to relapse into picaresque, with the stink of Mahood and Worm still in our nostrils. Now it's I the orator, the beleaguerers have departed, I am master on board, after the rats, I no longer crawl between the thwarts, under the moon, in the shadow of the lash, strange this mixture of solid and liquid, a little air now is all we need to complete the elements, no, I'm forgetting fire, unusual hell when you come to think of it, perhaps it's paradise, perhaps it's the earth, perhaps it's the shores of a lake beneath the earth, you scarcely breathe, but you breathe, it's not certain, you see nothing, hear nothing, you hear the long kiss of dead water and mud, aloft at less than a score of fathoms men come and go, you dream of them, in your long dream there's a place for the waking, you wonder how you know all you know, you even see grass, grass at dawn, glaucous with dew, not so blind as all that my eyes, they're not mine, mine are done, they don't even weep any more, they open and shut by the force of habit, fifteen minutes exposure, fifteen minutes shutter, like the owl cooped in the grotto in Battersea Park, ah misery, will I never stop wanting a life for myself? No no, no head either, anything you like, but not a head, in his head he doesn't go anywhere either, I've tried, lashed to the stake, blindfold, gagged to the gullet, you take the air, under the elms in se, murmuring Shelley, impervious to the shafts. Yes, a head, but solid, solid bone, and you imbedded in it, like a fossil in the rock. Perhaps there go I after all. I can't go on in any case. But I must go on. So I'll go on. Air, air, I'll seek air, air in time, the air of time, and in space, in my head, that's how I'll go on. All very fine, but the voice is failing, it's the first time, no, I've been through that, it has even stopped, many a time, that's how it will end again, I'll go silent, for want of air, then the voice will come back and I'll begin again. My voice. The voice. I hardly hear it any more. I'm going silent. Hearing this voice no more, that's what I call going silent. That is to say I'll hear it still, if I listen hard. I'll listen hard.

Listening hard, that's what I call going silent. I'll hear it still, broken, faint, unintelligible, if I listen hard. Hearing it still, without hearing what it says, that's what I call going silent. Then it will flare up, like a kindling fire, a dying fire, Mahood explained that to me, and I'll emerge from silence. Hearing too little to be able to speak, that's my silence. That is to say I never stop speaking, but sometimes too low, too far away, too far within, to hear, no, I hear, to understand, not that I ever understand. It fades, it goes in, behind the door, I'm going silent, there's going to be silence, I'll listen, it's worse than speaking, no, no worse, no better. Unless this time it's the true silence, the one I'll never have to break any more, when I won't have to listen any more, when I can dribble in my corner, my head gone, my tongue dead, the one I have tried to earn, that I thought I could earn. I'm going to stop, that is to say I'm going to look as if I had, it will be like everything else. As if anyone were looking at me! As if it were I! It will be the same silence, the same as ever, murmurous with muted lamentation, panting and exhaling of impossible sorrow, like distant laughter, and brief spells of hush, as of one buried before his time. Long or short, the same silence. Then I resurrect and begin again. That's what I'll have got for all my pains. Unless this time it's the real silence at last. Perhaps I've said the thing that had to be said, that gives me the right to be done with speech, done with listening, done with hearing, without my knowing it. I'm listening already, I'm going silent. The next time I won't go to such pains, I'll tell one of Mahood's old tales, no matter which, they are all alike, they won't tire me, I won't bother any more about me, I'll know that no matter what I say the result is the same, that I'll never be silent, never at peace. Unless I try once more, just once more, one last time, to say what has to be said, about me, I feel it's about me, perhaps that's the mistake I make, perhaps that's my sin, so as to have nothing more to say, nothing more to hear, till I die. It's coming back. I'm glad. I'll try again, quick before it goes again. Try what? I don't know. To continue. Now there is no one left. That's a good continuation. No one left, it's embarrassing, if I had a memory it might tell me that this is the sign of the end, this having no one left, no one to talk to, no one to talk to you, so that you have to say, It's I who am doing this to me, I who am talking to me about me. Then the breath fails, the end begins, you go silent, it's the end, short-lived, you begin again, you had forgotten, there's someone there, someone talking to you, about you, about him, then a second, then a third, then the second again, then all three together, these figures just to give you an idea, talking to you, about you, about them, all I have to do is listen, then they depart, one by one, and the voice goes on, it's not theirs, they were never there, there was never anyone but you, talking to you about you, the breath fails, it's nearly the end, the breath stops, it's the end, shortlived, I hear someone calling me, it begins again, that must be how it goes, if I had a memory. Even if there were things, a thing somewhere, a scrap of nature, to talk about, you might be reconciled to having no one left, to being yourself the talker, if only there were a thing somewhere, to talk about, even though you couldn't see it, or know what it was, simply feel it there, with you, you might have the courage not to go silent, no, it's to go silent that you need courage, for you'll be punished, punished for having gone silent, and yet you can't do otherwise than go silent, than be punished for having gone silent, than be punished for having been punished, since you begin again, the breath fails, if only there were a thing, but there it is, there is not, they took away things when they departed, they took away nature, there was never anyone, anyone but me, anything but me, talking to me of me, impossible to stop, impossible to go on, but I must go on, I'll go on, without anyone, without anything, but me, but my voice, that is to say I'll stop, I'll end, it's the end already, short-lived, what is it, a little hole, you go down into it, into the silence, it's worse than the noise, you listen, it's worse than talking, no, not worse, no worse, you wait, in anguish, have they forgotten me, no, yes, no, someone calls me, I crawl out again, what is it, a little hole, in the wilderness. It's the end that is the worst, no, it's the beginning that is the worst, then the middle, then the end, in the end it's the end that is the worst, this voice that, I don't know, it's every second that is the worst, it's a chronicle, the seconds pass, one after another, jerkily, no flow, they don't pass, they arrive, bang, bang, they bang into you, bounce off, fall and never move again, when you have nothing left to say you talk of time, seconds of time, there are some people add them together to make a life, I can't, each one is the first, no, the second, or the third, I'm three seconds old, oh not every day of the week. I've been away, done something, been in a hole, I've just crawled out, perhaps I went silent, no, I say that in order to say something, in order to go on a little more, you must go on a little more, you must go on a long time more, you must go on evermore, if I could remember what I have said I could repeat it, if I could learn something by heart I'd be saved, I have to keep on saying the same thing and each time it's an effort, the seconds must be alike and each one is infernal, what am I saying now, I'm saying I wish I knew. And yet I have memories, I remember Worm, that is to say I have retained the name, and the other, what is his name, what was his name, in his jar, I can see him still, better than I can see me, I know how he lived, now I remember, I alone saw him, but no one sees me, nor him, I don't see him any more, Mahood, he was called Mahood, I don't see him any more, I don't know how he lived any more, he isn't there any more, he was never there, in his jar, I never saw him, and yet I remember, I remember having talked about him, I must have talked about him, the same words recur and they are your memories. It is I invented him, him and so many others, and the places where they passed, the places where they stayed, in order to speak, since I had to speak, without speaking of me, I couldn't speak of me, I was never told I had to speak of me, I invented my memories, not knowing what I was doing, not one is of me. It is they asked me to speak of them, they wanted to know what they were, how they lived, that suited me, I thought that would suit me, since I had nothing to say and had to say something, I thought I was free to say any old thing, so long as I didn't go silent. Then I said to myself that after all perhaps it wasn't any old thing, the thing I was saying, that it might well be the thing demanded of me, assuming something was being demanded of me. No, I didn't think anything and I didn't say anything to myself, I did what I could, a thing beyond my strength, and often for exhaustion I gave up doing it, and yet it went on being done, the voice being heard, the voice which could not be mine, since I had none left, and yet which could only be mine, since I could not go silent, and since I was alone, in a place where no voice could reach me. Yes, in my life, since we must call it so, there were three things, the inability to speak, the inability to be silent, and solitude, that's what I've had to make the best of. Yes, now I can speak of my life, I'm too tired for niceties, but I don't know if I ever lived, I have really no opinion on the subject. However that may be I think I'll soon go silent for good, in spite of its being prohibited. Then, yes, phut, just like that, just like one of the living, then I'll be dead, I think I'll soon be dead, I hope I find it a change. I should have liked to go silent first, there were moments I thought that would be my reward for having spoken so long and so valiantly, to enter living into silence, so as to be able to enjoy it, no, I don't know why, so as to feel myself silent, one with all this quiet air shattered unceasingly by my voice alone, no, it's not real air, I can't say it, I can't say why I should have liked to be silent a little before being dead, so as in the end to be a little as I always was and never could be, without fear of worse to come peacefully in the place where I always was and could never rest in peace, no, I don't know, it's simpler than that, I wanted myself, in my own land for a brief space, I didn't want to die a stranger in the midst of strangers, a stranger in my own midst, surrounded by invaders, no, I don't know what I wanted, I don't know what I thought, I must have wanted so many things, imagined so many things, while I was talking, without knowing exactly what, enough to go blind, with longings and visions, mingling and merging in one another, I'd have been better employed minding what I was saying. But it didn't happen like that, it happened like this, the way it's happening now, that is to say, I don't know, you mustn't believe what I'm saying, I don't know what I'm saying, I'm doing as I always did, I'm going on as best I can. As to believing I shall go silent for good and all, I don't believe it particularly, I always believed it, as I always believed I would never go silent, you can't call that believing, it's my walls. But has nothing really changed, all this time? If instead of having something to say I had something to do, with my hands or feet, some little job, sorting things for example, or simply arranging things, suppose for the sake of argument I had the job of moving things from one place to another, then I'd know where I was, and how far I had got, no, not necessarily, I can see it from here, they would contrive things in such a way that I couldn't suspect the two vessels, the one to be emptied and the one to be filled, of being in reality one and the same, it would be water, water, with my thimble I'd go and draw it from one container and then I'd go and pour it into another, or there would be four, or a hundred, half of them to be filled, the other half to be emptied, numbered, the even to be emptied, the uneven to be filled, no, it would be more complicated, less symmetrical, no matter, to be emptied, and filled, in a certain way, a certain order, in accordance with certain homologies, the word is not too strong, so that I'd have to think, tanks, communicating, communicating, connected by pipes under the floor, I can see it from here, always showing the same level, no, that wouldn't work, too hopeless, they'd arrange for me to have little attacks of hope from time to time, yes, pipes and taps, I can see it from here, so that I might fool myself from time to time, if I had that to do, instead of this, some little job with fluids, filling and emptying, always the same vessel, I'd be good at that, it would be a better life than this, no, I mustn't start complaining, I'd have a body, I wouldn't have to speak, I'd hear my steps, almost without ceasing, and the noise of the water, and the crying of the air trapped in the pipes, I don't under-stand, I'd have bouts of zeal, I'd say to myself, The quicker I do it the quicker it will be done, the things one has to listen to, that's where hope would come in, it wouldn't be dark, impossible to do such work in the dark, that depends, yes, I must say I see no window, from here, whereas here that has no importance, that I see no window, here I needn't come and go, fortunately, I couldn't, nor be dextrous, for naturally the water would have great value and the least drop spilt on the way, or in the act of drawing, or in the act of pouring, would cost me dear, and how could you tell, in the dark, if a drop, what's this story, it's a story, now I've told another little story, about me, about the life that might have been mine for all the difference it would have made, which was perhaps mine, perhaps I went through that before being deemed worthy of going through this, who knows towards what high destiny I am heading, unless I am coming from it. But once again the fable must be of another, I see him so well, coming and going among his casks, trying to stop his hand from trembling, dropping his thimble, listening to it bouncing and rolling on the floor, scraping round for it with his foot, going down on his knees, going down on his belly, crawling, it stops there, it must have been I, but I never saw myself, so it can't have been I, I don't know, how can I recognise myself who never made my acquaintance, it stops there, that's all I know, I don't see him any more, I'll never see him again, yes I will, now he's there with the others, I won't name them again, you say that for something to say, you say anything for something to say, some do this, others that, he does as I said, I don't remember, he'll come back, to keep me company, only the wicked are solitary, I'll see him again, it's his fault, his fault for wanting to know what he was like, and how he lived, or he'll never come back, it's one or the other, they don't all come back, I mean there must be some I have only seen once, up to now, very true, it's only beginning, I feel the end at hand and the beginning likewise, to every man his orbit, that's obvious. But, and here I return to the charge, but has nothing really changed, all this mortal time, I'm speaking now of me, yes, henceforward I shall speak of none but me, that's decided, even though I should not succeed, there's no reason why I should succeed, so I need have no qualms. Nothing changed? I must be ageing all the same, bah, I was always aged, always ageing, and ageing makes no difference, not to mention that all this is not about me, hell, I've contradicted myself, no matter. So long as one does not know what one is saying and can't stop to inquire, in tranquillity, fortunately, fortunately, one would like to stop, but unconditionally, I resume, so long as, so long as, let me see, so long as one, so long as he, ah fuck all that, so long as this, then that, agreed, that's good enough, I nearly got stuck. Help, help, if I could only describe this place, I who am so good at describing places, walls, ceilings, floors, they are my speciality, doors, windows, what haven't I imagined in the way of windows in the course of my career, some opened on the sea, all you could see was sea and sky, if I could put myself in a room, that would be the end of the wordy-gurdy, even doorless, even windowless, nothing but the four surfaces, the six surfaces, if I could shut myself up, it would be a mine, it could be black dark, I could be motionless and fixed, I'd find a way to explore it, I'd listen to the echo, I'd get to know it, I'd get to remember it, I'd be home, I'd say what it's like, in my home, instead of any old thing, this place, if I could describe this place, portray it, I've tried, I feel no place, no place round me, there's no end to me, I don't know what it is, it isn't flesh, it doesn't end, it's like air, now I have it, you say that, to say something, you won't say it long, like gas, balls, balls, the place, then we'll see, first the place, then I'll find me in it, I'll put me in it, a solid lump, in the middle, or in a corner, well propped up on three sides, the place, if only I could feel a place for me, I've tried, I'll try again, none was ever mine, that sea under my window, higher than the window, and the row-boat, do you remember, and the river, and the bay, I knew I had memories, pity they are not of me, and the stars, and the beacons, and the lights of the buoys, and the mountain burning, it was the time nothing was too good for me, the others benefited by it, they died like flies, or the forest, a roof is not indispensable, an interior, if I could be in a forest, caught in a thicket, or wandering round in circles, it would be the end of this blither, I'd describe the leaves, one by one, at the moment of their growing, at the moment of their giving shade, at the moment of their falling, those are good moments, for one who has not to say, But it's not I, it's not I, where am I, what am I doing, all this time, as if that mattered, but there it is, that takes the heart out of you, your heart isn't in it any more, your heart that was, among the brambles, cradled by the shadows, you try the sea, you try the town, you look for yourself in the mountains and the plains, it's only natural, you want yourself, you want yourself in your own little corner, it's not love, not curiosity, it's because you're tired, you want to stop, travel no more, seek no more, lie no more, speak no more, close your eyes, but your own, in a word lay your hands on yourself, after that you'll make short work of it. I notice one thing, the others have vanished, completely, I don't like it. Notice, I notice nothing, I go on as best I can, if it begins to mean something I can't help it, I have passed by here, this has passed by me, thousands of times, its turn has come again, it will pass on and something else will be there, another instant of my old instant, there it is, the old meaning that I'll give myself, that I won't be able to give myself, there's a god for the damned, as on the first day, today is the first day, it begins, I know it well, I'll remember it as I go along, all adown it I'll be born and born, births for nothing, and come to night without having been. Look at this Tunis pink, it's dawn. If I could only shut myself up, quick, I'll shut myself up, it won't be I, quick, I'll make a place, it won't be mine, it doesn't matter, I don't feel any place for me, perhaps that will come, I'll make it mine, I'll put myself in it, I'll put someone in it, I'll find someone in it, I'll put myself in him, I'll say he's I, perhaps he'll keep me, perhaps the place will keep us, me inside the other, the place all round us, it will be over, all over, I won't have to try and move any more, I'll close my eyes, all I'll have to do is talk, that will be easy, I'll have things to say, about me, about my life, I'll make it a good one, I'll know who's talking, and about what, I'll know where I am, perhaps I'll be able to go silent, perhaps that's all they're waiting for, there they are again, to pardon me, waiting for me to reach home, to pardon me, it's the lie they refuse to stop, I'll close my eyes, be happy at last, that's the way it is this morning. Morning, I call that morning, that's right, shilly-shally a little longer, I call that morning, I haven't many words, I haven't much choice, I don't choose, the word came, I should have avoided this bright stain, it's the dayspring, but it doesn't last, I know it, I call that the dayspring, if you could only see it. I'm off, you wouldn't think so, perhaps it's my last gallop, I smell the stable, I always smelt the stable, it's I smell of the stable, there's no stable but me, for me. No, I won't do it, what won't I do, as if that depended on me, I won't seek my home any more, I don't know what I'll do, it would be occupied already, there would be someone there already, someone far gone, he wouldn't want me, I can understand him, I'd disturb him, what am I going to say now, I'm going to ask myself, I'm going to ask questions, that's a good stop-gap, not that I'm in any danger of stopping, then why all this fuss, that's right, questions, I know millions, I must know millions, and then there are plans, when questions fail there are always plans, you say what you'll say and what you won't say, that doesn't commit you to anything and the evil moment passes, it drops stone dead, suddenly you hear yourself talking about God knows what as if you had done nothing else all your life, and neither have you, you come back from a far place, back to life, that's where you should be, where you are, far from here, far from everything, if only I could go there, if only I could describe it, I who am so good at topography, that's right, aspirations, when plans fail there are always aspirations, it's a knack, you must say it slowly, If only this, if only that, that gives you time, time for a cud of longing to rise up in the back of your gullet, nothing remains but to look as if you enjoyed chewing it, there's no knowing where that may lead you, on tracks as beaten as the day is long, often you pass yourself by, someone passes himself by, if only you knew, that's right, aspirations, you turn and look behind you, so does the other, you weep for him, he weeps for you, it's screamingly sad, anything rather than laughter. What else, opinions, comparisons, anything rather than laughter, all helps, can't help helping, to get you over the pretty pass, the things you have to listen to, what pretty pass, it's not I speaking, it's not I hearing, let us not go into that, let us go on as if I were the only one in the world, whereas I'm the only one absent from it, or with others, what difference does it make, others present, others absent, they are not obliged to make themselves manifest, all that is needed is to wander and let wander, be this slow boundless whirlwind and every particle of its dust, it's impossible. Someone speaks, someone hears, no need to go any further, it is not he, it's I, or another, or others, what does it matter, the case is clear, it is not he, he who I know I am, that's all I know, who I cannot say I am, I can't say anything, I've tried, I'm trying, he knows nothing, knows of nothing, neither what it is to speak, nor what it is to hear, to know nothing, to be capable of nothing, and to have to try, you don't try any more, no need to try, it goes on by itself, it drags on by itself, from word to word, a labouring whirl, you are in it somewhere, everywhere, not he, if only I could forget him, have one second of this noise that carries me away, without having to say, I don't, I haven't time, It's not I, I am he, after all, why not, why not say it, I must have said it, as well that as anything else, it's not I, not I, I can't say it, it came like that, it comes like that, it's not I, if only it could be about him, if only it could come about him, I'd deny him, with pleasure, if that could help, it's I, here it's I, speak to me of him, let me speak of him, that's all I ask, I never asked for anything, make

188

me speak of him, what a mess, now there is no one left, long may it last. In the end it comes to that, to the survival of that alone, then the words come back, someone says I, unbelieving. If only I could make an effort, an effort of attention, to try and discover what's happening, what's happening to me, what then, I don't know, I've forgotten my apodosis, but I can't, I don't hear any more, I'm sleeping, they call that sleeping, there they are again, we'll have to start killing them again, I hear this horrible noise, coming back takes time, I don't know where from, I was nearly there, I was nearly sleeping, I call that sleeping, there is no one but me, there was never anyone but me, here I mean, elsewhere is another matter, I was never elsewhere, here is my only elsewhere, it's I who do this thing and I who suffer it, it's not possible otherwise, it's not possible so, it's not my fault, all I can say is that it's not my fault, it's not anyone's fault, since there isn't anyone it can't be anyone's fault, since there isn't anyone but me it can't be mine, sometimes you'd think I was reasoning, I've no objection, they must have taught me reasoning too, they must have begun teaching me, before they deserted me, I don't remember that period, but it must have marked me, I don't remember having been deserted, perhaps I received a shock. Strange, these phrases that die for no reason, strange, what's strange about it, here all is strange, all is strange when you come to think of it, no, it's coming to think of it that is strange, am I to suppose I am inhabited, I can't suppose anything, I have to go on, that's what I'm doing, let others suppose, there must be others in other elsewheres, each one in his little elsewhere, this word that keeps coming back, each one saying to himself, when the moment comes, the moment to say it, Let others suppose, and so on, so on, let others do this, others do that, if there are any, that helps you on, that helps you forward, I believe in progress, I know how to believe too, they must have taught me believing too, no, no one ever taught me anything, I never learnt anything, I've always been here, here there was never anyone but me, never, always, me, no one, old slush to be churned everlastingly, now it's slush, a minute ago it was dust, it must have rained. He must have travelled, he whose voice it is, he must have seen, with his eyes, a man or two, a thing or two, been aloft, in the light, or else heard tales, travellers found him and told him tales, that proves my innocence, who says, That proves my innocence, he says it, or they say it, yes, they who reason, they who believe, no, in the singular, he who lived, or saw some who had, he speaks of me, as if I were he, as if I were not he, both, and as if I were others, one after another, he is the afflicted, I am far, do you hear him, he says I'm far, as if I were he, no, as if I were not he, for he is not far, he is here, it's he who speaks, he says it's I, then he says it's not, I am far, do you hear him, he seeks me I don't know why, he doesn't know why, he calls me, he wants me to come out, he thinks I can come out, he wants me to be he, or another, let us be fair, he wants me to rise up, up into him, or up into another, let us be impartial, he thinks he's caught me, he feels me in him, then he says I, as if I were he, or in another, let us be just, then he says Murphy, or Molloy, I forget, as if I were Malone, but their day is done, he wants none but himself, for me, he thinks it's his last chance, he thinks that, they taught him thinking, it's always he who speaks, Mercier never spoke, Moran never spoke, I never spoke, I seem to speak, that's because he says I as if he were I, I nearly believed him, do you hear him, as if he were I, I who am far, who can't move, can't be found, but neither can he, he can only talk, if that much, perhaps it's not he, perhaps it's a multitude, one after another, what confusion, someone mentions confusion, is it a sin, all here is sin, you don't know why, you don't know whose, you don't know against whom, someone says you, it's the fault of the pronouns, there is no name for me, no pronoun for me, all the trouble comes from that, that, it's a kind of pronoun too, it isn't that either, I'm not that either, let us leave all that, forget about all that, it's not difficult, our concern is with someone, or our concern is with something, now we're getting it, someone or something that is not there, or that is not anywhere, or that is there, here, why not, after all, and our concern is with speaking of that, now we've got it, you don't know why, why you must speak of that, but there it is, you can't speak of that, no one can speak of that, you speak of yourself, someone speaks of himself, that's it, in the singular, a single one, the man on duty, he, I, no matter, the man on duty speaks of himself, it's not that, of others, it's not that either, he doesn't know, how could he know, whether he has spoken of that or not, when speaking of himself, when speaking of others, when speaking of things, how can I know, I can't know, if I've spoken of him, I can only speak of me, no, I can't speak of anything, and yet I speak, perhaps it's of him, I'll never know, how could I know, who could know, who knowing could tell me, I don't know who it's all about, that's all I know, no, I must know something else, they must have taught me something, it's about him who knows nothing, wants nothing, can do nothing, if it's possible you can do nothing when you want nothing, who cannot hear, cannot speak, who is I, who cannot be I, of whom I can't speak, of whom I must speak, that's all hypotheses, I said nothing, someone said nothing, it's not a question of hypotheses, it's a question of going on, it goes on, hypotheses are like everything else, they help you on, as if there were need of help, that's right, impersonal, as if there were any need of help to go on with a thing that can't stop, and yet it will, it will stop, do you hear, the voice says it will stop, some day, it says it will stop and it says it will never stop, fortunately I have no opinion, what would I have an opinion with, with my mouth perhaps, if it's mine, I don't feel a mouth on me, that means nothing, if only I could feel a mouth on me, if only I could feel something on me, I'll try, if I can, I know it's not I, that's all I know, I say I, knowing it's not I, I am far, far, what does that mean, far, no need to be far, perhaps he's here, in my arms, I don't feel any arms on me, if only I could feel something on me, it would be a starting-point, a starting-point, ah if I could laugh, I know what it is, they must have told me what it is, but I can't do it, they can't have shown me how to do it, perhaps it's one of those gifts that can't be acquired. The silence, a word on the silence, in the silence, that's the worst, to speak of silence, then lock me up, lock someone up, that is to say, what is that to say, calm, calm, I'm calm, I'm locked up, I'm in something, it's not I, that's all I know, no more about that, that is to say, make a place, a little world, it will be round, this time it will be round, it's not certain, low of ceiling, thick of wall, why low, why thick, I don't know, it isn't certain, it remains to be seen, all remains to be seen, a little world, try and find out what it's like, try and guess, put someone in it, seek someone in it, and what he's like, and how he manages, it won't be I, no matter, perhaps it will, perhaps it will be my world, possible coincidence, there won't be windows, we're done with windows, the sea refused me, the sky didn't see me, I wasn't there, and the summer evening air weighing on my eyelids, we must have eyelids, we must have eyeballs, it's preferable, they must have explained to me, someone must have explained to me, what it's like, an eye, at the window, before the sea, before the earth, before the sky, at the window, against the air, opening, shutting, grey, black, grey, black, I must have understood, I must have wanted it, wanted the eye, for my own, I must have tried, all the things they've told me, all the things I've tried, they come in useful still, when I think of them, that too, you must go on thinking too, the old thoughts, they call that thinking, it's visions, shreds of old visions, that's all you can see, a few old pictures, a window, what need had they to show me a window, saying, no, I forget, it doesn't come back to me, a window, saying, There are others, even more beautiful, and the rest, walls, sky, man, like Mahood, a little nature, too long to go over, too forgotten, too little forgotten, was it necessary, but was that how it happened, who can have come here, the devil perhaps, I can think of no one else, it's he showed me everything, here, in the dark, and how to speak, and what to say, and a little nature, and a few names, and the outside of men, those in my image, whom I might resemble, and their way of living, in rooms, in sheds, in caverns, in woods, or coming and going, I forget, and who went away and left me, knowing I was tempted, knowing I was lost, whether I succumbed or not, have I succumbed or not, I don't know, it's not I, that's all I know, since that day it's not I any more, since that day there is no one any more, I must have succumbed. That's all hypotheses, that helps you forward, I believe in progress, I believe in silence, ah yes, a few words on the silence, then the little world, that will be enough, for the rest of eternity, you'd think it was I, I speaking, I hearing, I making plans, for the passing hour, for the rest of eternity, whereas I'm far, or in my arms somewhere, or stowed away somewhere, behind walls, a few words on the silence, then just one thing more, just one space and someone within, perhaps, until the end, I believe it, it's evening already, I call that evening, I wish you could see it, I believe it this evening, it's announced and I believe it, you announce, then you renounce, so it is, that helps you on, that helps the end to come, evenings when there is an end, I speak of evening, someone speaks of evening, perhaps it's still morning, perhaps it's still night, personally I have no opinion. They love each other, marry, in order to love each other better, more conveniently, he goes to the wars, he dies at the wars, she weeps, with emotion, at having

195

loved him, at having lost him, yep, marries again, in
order to love again, more conveniently again, they love
each other, you love as many times as necessary, as
necessary in order to be happy, he comes back, the
other comes back, from the wars, he didn't die at the
wars after all, she goes to the station, to meet him, he
dies in the train, of emotion, at the thought of seeing
her again, having her again, she weeps, weeps again,
with emotion again, at having lost him again, yep, goes
back to the house, he's dead, the other is dead, the
mother-in-law takes him down, he hanged himself,
with emotion, at the thought of losing her, she weeps,
weeps louder, at having loved him, at having lost him,
there's a story for you, that was to teach me the nature
of emotion, that's called emotion, what emotion can do,
given favourable conditions, what love can do, well
well, so that's emotion, that's love, and trains, the nature
of trains, and the meaning of your back to the engine,
and guards, stations, platforms, wars, love, heart-
rending cries, that must be the mother-in-law, her cries
rend the heart as she takes down her son, or her son-in-
law, I don't know, it must be her son, since she cries,
and the door, the house-door is bolted, when she got
back from the station she found the house-door bolted,
who bolted it, he the better to hang himself, or the
mother-in-law the better to take him down, or to
prevent her daughter-in-law from re-entering the

premises, there's a story for you, it must be the daughter-in-law, it isn't the son-in-law and the daughter, it's the daughter-in-law and the son, how I reason to be sure this evening, it was to teach me how to reason, it was to tempt me to go, to the place where you can come to an end, I must have been a good pupil up to a point, I couldn't get beyond a certain point, I can understand their annoyance, this evening I begin to understand, oh there's no danger, it's not I, it wasn't I, the door, it's the door interests me, a wooden door, who bolted the door, and for what purpose, I'll never know, there's a story for you, I thought they were over, perhaps it's a new one, lepping fresh, is it the return to the world of fable, no, just a reminder, to make me regret what I have lost, long to be again in the place I was banished from, unfortunately it doesn't remind me of anything. The silence, speak of the silence before going into it, was I there already, I don't know, at every instant I'm there, listen to me speaking of it, I knew it would come, I emerge from it to speak of it, I stay in it to speak of it, if it's I who speak, and it's not, I act as if it were, sometimes I act as if it were, but at length, was I ever there at length, a long stay, I understand nothing about duration, I can't speak of it, oh I know I speak of it, I say never and ever, I speak of the four seasons and the different parts of the day and night, the night has no parts, that's because you are asleep, the seasons must be very similar, perhaps it's spring-time now, that's all words they taught me, without making their meaning clear to me, that's how I learnt to reason, I use them all, all the words they showed me, there were columns of them, oh the strange glow all of a sudden, they were on lists, with images opposite, I must have forgotten them, I must have mixed them up, these nameless images I have, these imageless names, these windows I should perhaps rather call doors, at least by some other name, and this word man which is perhaps not the right one for the thing I see when I hear it, but an instant, an hour, and so on, how can they be represented, a life, how could that be made clear to me, here, in the dark, I call that the dark, perhaps it's azure, blank words, but I use them, they keep coming back, all those they showed me, all those I remember, I need them all, to be able to go on, it's a lie, a score would be plenty, tried and trusty, unforget-table, nicely varied, that would be palette enough, I'd mix them, I'd vary them, that would be gamut enough, all the things I'd do if I could, if I wished, if I could wish, no need to wish, that's how it will end, in heart-rending cries, inarticulate murmurs, to be invented, as I go along, improvised, as I groan along, I'll laugh, that's how it will end, in a chuckle, chuck chuck, ow, ha, pa, I'll practise, nyum, hoo, plop, psss, nothing but emotion, bing bang, that's blows, ugh, pooh, what else, oooh, aaah, that's love, enough, it's tiring, hee hee, that's the Abderite, no, the other, in the end, it's the end, the ending end, it's the silence, a few gurgles on the silence, the real silence, not the one where I macerate up to the mouth, up to the ear, that covers me, uncovers me, breathes with me, like a cat with a mouse, that of the drowned, I've drowned, more than once, it wasn't I, suffocated, set fire to me, thumped on my head with wood and iron, it wasn't I, there was no head, no wood, no iron, I didn't do anything to me, I didn't do anything to anyone, no one did anything to me, there is no one, I've looked, no one but me, no, not me either, I've looked everywhere, there must be someone, the voice must belong to someone, I've no objection, what it wants I want, I am it, I've said so, it says so, from time to time it says so, then it says not, I've no objection, I want it to go silent, it wants to go silent, it can't, it does for a second, then it starts again, that's not the real silence, it says that's not the real silence, what can be said of the real silence, I don't know, that I don't know what it is, that there is no such thing, that perhaps there is such a thing, yes, that perhaps there is, somewhere, I'll never know. But when it falters and when it stops, but it falters every instant, it stops every instant, yes, but when it stops for a good few moments, a good few moments, what are a good few moments, what then, murmurs, then it must be murmurs, and listening, someone listening, no need of an ear, no need of a mouth, the voice listens, as when it speaks, listens to its silence, that makes a murmur, that makes a voice, a small voice, the same voice only small, it sticks in the throat, there's the throat again, there's the mouth again, it fills the ear, there's the ear again, then I vomit, someone vomits, someone starts vomiting again, that must be how it happens, I have no explanations to offer, none to demand, the comma will come where I'll drown for good, then the silence, I believe it this evening, still this evening, how it drags on, I've no objection, perhaps it's springtime, violets, no, that's autumn, there's a time for everything, for the things that pass, the things that end, they could never get me to understand that, the things that stir, depart, return, a light changing, they could never get me to see that, and death into the bargain, a voice dying, that's a good one, silence at last, not a murmur, no air, no one listening, not for the likes of me, amen, on we go. Enormous prison, like a hundred thousand cathedrals, never anything else any more, from this time forth, and in it, somewhere, perhaps, riveted, tiny, the prisoner, how can he be found, how false this space is, what falseness instantly, to want to draw that round you, to want to put a being there, a cell would be plenty, if I gave up, if only I could give up, before beginning, before beginning again, what breathlessness, that's right, ejaculations, that helps you on, that puts off the fatal hour, no, the reverse, I don't know, start again, in this immensity, this obscurity, go through the motions of starting again, you who can't stir, you who never started, you the who, go through the motions, what motions, you can't stir, you launch your voice, it dies away in the vault, it calls that a vault, perhaps it's the abyss, those are words, it speaks of a prison, I've no objection, vast enough for a whole people, for me alone, or waiting for me, I'll go there now, I'll try and go there now, I can't stir, I'm there already, I must be there already, perhaps I'm not alone, perhaps a whole people is here, and the voice its voice, coming to me fitfully, we would have lived, been free a moment, now we talk about it, each one to himself, each one out loud for himself, and we listen, a whole people, talking and listening, all together, that would ex, no, I'm alone, perhaps the first, or perhaps the last, talking alone, listening alone, alone alone, the others are gone, they have been stilled, their voices stilled, their listening stilled, one by one, at each new-coming, another will come, I won't be the last, I'll be with the others, I'll be as gone, in the silence, it won't be I, it's not I, I'm not there yet, I'll go there now, I'll try and go there now, no use trying, I wait for my turn, my turn to go there, my turn to talk there, my turn to listen there, my turn to wait there for my turn to go, to be as gone, it's unending, it will be unending, gone

where, where do you go from there, you must go somewhere else, wait somewhere else, for your turn to go
again, and so on, a whole people, or I alone, and come
back, and begin again, no, go on, go on again, it's a
circuit, a long circuit, I know it well, I must know it
well, it's a lie, I can't stir, I haven't stirred, I launch the
voice, I hear a voice, there is nowhere but here, there
are not two places, there are not two prisons, it's my
parlour, it's a parlour, where I wait for nothing, I don't
know where it is, I don't know what it's like, that's no
business of mine, I don't know if it's big, or if it's small,
or if it's closed, if it's open, that's right, reiterate, that
helps you on, open on what, there is nothing else, only
it, open on the void, open on the nothing, I've no
objection, those are words, open on the silence, looking
out on the silence, straight out, why not, all this time on
the brink of silence, I knew it, on a rock, lashed to a
rock, in the midst of silence, its great swell rears towards
me, I'm streaming with it, it's an image, those are
words, it's a body, it's not I, I knew it wouldn't be I, I'm
not outside, I'm inside, I'm in something, I'm shut up,
the silence is outside, outside, inside, there is nothing
but here, and the silence outside, nothing but this
voice and the silence all round, no need of walls, yes,
we must have walls, I need walls, good and thick, I
need a prison, I was right, for me alone, I'll go there
now, I'll put me in it, I'm there already, I'll start looking

for me now, I'm there somewhere, it won't be I, no matter, I'll say it's I, perhaps it will be I, perhaps that's all they're waiting for, there they are again, to give me quittance, waiting for me to say I'm someone, to say I'm somewhere, to put me out, into the silence, I see nothing, it's because there is nothing, or it's because I have no eyes, or both, that makes three possibilities, to choose from, but do I really see nothing, it's not the moment to tell a lie, but how can you not tell a lie, what an idea, a voice like this, who can check it, it tries everything, it's blind, it seeks me blindly, in the dark, it seeks a mouth, to enter into, who can query it, there is no other, you'd need a head, you'd need things, I don't know, I look too often as if I knew, it's the voice does that, it goes all knowing, to make me think I know, to make me think it's mine, it has no interest in eyes, it says I have none, or that they are no use to me, then it speaks of tears, then it speaks of gleams, it is truly at a loss, gleams, yes, far, or near, distances, you know, measurements, enough said, gleams, as at dawn, then dying, as at evening, or flaring up, they do that too, blaze up more dazzling than snow, for a second, that's short, then fizzle out, that's true enough, if you like, one forgets, I forget, I say I see nothing, or I say it's all in my head, as if I felt a head on me, that's all hypotheses, lies, these gleams too, they were to save me, they were to devour me, that came to nothing, I see nothing, either because of this or else on account of that, and these images at which they watered me, like a camel, before the desert, I don't know, more lies, just for the fun of it, fun, what fun we've had, what fun of it, all lies, that's soon said, you must say soon, it's the regulations. The place, I'll make it all the same, I'll make it in my head, I'll draw it out of my memory, I'll gather it all about me, I'll make myself a head, I'll make myself a memory, I have only to listen, the voice will tell me everything, tell it to me again, everything I need, in dribs and drabs, breathless, it's like a confession, a last confession, you think it's finished, then it starts off again, there were so many sins, the memory is so bad, the words don't come, the words fail, the breath fails, no, it's something else, it's an indictment, a dying voice accusing, accusing me, you must accuse someone, a culprit is indispensable, it speaks of my sins, it speaks of my head, it says it's mine, it says that I repent, that I want to be punished, better than I am, that I want to go, give myself up, a victim is essential, I have only to listen, it will show me my hiding-place, what it's like, where the door is, if there's a door, and whereabouts I am in it, and what lies between us, how the land lies, what kind of country, whether it's sea, or whether it's mountain, and the way to take, so that I may go, make my escape, give myself up, come to the place where the axe falls, without further ceremony, on all who come from here, I'm not the first, I won't be the first, it will best me in the end, it has bested better than me, it will tell me what to do, in order to rise, move, act like a body endowed with despair, that's how I reason, that's how I hear myself reasoning, all lies, it's not me they're calling, not me they're talking about, it's not yet my turn, it's someone else's turn, that's why I can't stir, that's why I don't feel a body on me, I'm not suffering enough yet, it's not yet my turn, not suffering enough to be able to stir, to have a body, complete with head, to be able to understand, to have eyes to light the way, I merely hear, without understanding, without being able to profit by it, by what I hear, to do what, to rise and go and be done with hearing, I don't hear everything, that must be it, the important things escape me, it's not my turn, the topographical and anatomical information in particular is lost on me, no, I hear everything, what difference does it make, the moment it's not my turn, my turn to understand, my turn to live, my turn of the life-screw, it calls that living, the space of the way from here to the door, it's all there, in what I hear, somewhere, if all has been said, all this long time, all must have been said, but it's not my turn to know what, to know what I am, where I am, and what I should do to stop being it, to stop being there, that's coherent, so as to be another, no, the same, I don't know, depart into life, travel the road, find the door, find the axe, perhaps it's a cord, for the neck, for the throat, for the cords, or fingers, I'll have eyes, I'll see fingers, it will be the silence, perhaps it's a drop, find the door, open the door, drop, into the silence, it won't be I, I'll stay here, or there, more likely there, it will never be I, that's all I know, it's all been done already, said and said again, the departure, the body that rises, the way, in colour, the arrival, the door that opens, closes again, it was never I, I've never stirred, I've listened, I must have spoken, why deny it, why not admit it, after all, I deny nothing, I admit nothing, I say what I hear, I hear what I say, I don't know, one or the other, or both, that makes three possibilities, pick your fancy, all these stories about travellers, these stories about paralytics, all are mine, I must be extremely old, or it's memory playing tricks, if only I knew if I've lived, if I live, if I'll live, that would simplify everything, impossible to find out, that's where you're buggered, I haven't stirred, that's all I know, no, I know something else, it's not I, I always forget that, I resume, you must resume, never stirred from here, never stopped telling stories, to myself, hardly hearing them, hearing something else, listening for something else, wondering now and then where I got them from, was I in the land of the living, were they in mine, and where, where do I store them, in my head, I don't feel a head on me, and what do I tell them with, with my mouth, same remark, and what do I hear them

206

with, and so on, the old rigmarole, it can't be I, or it's because I pay no heed, it's such an old habit, I do it without heeding, or as if I were somewhere else, there I am far again, there I am the absentee again, it's his turn again now, he who neither speaks nor listens, who has neither body nor soul, it's something else he has, he must have something, he must be somewhere, he is made of silence, there's a pretty analysis, he's in the silence, he's the one to be sought, the one to be, the one to be spoken of, the one to speak, but he can't speak, then I could stop, I'd be he, I'd be the silence, I'd be back in the silence, we'd be reunited, his story the story to be told, but he has no story, he hasn't been in story, it's not certain, he's in his own story, unimaginable, unspeakable, that doesn't matter, the attempt must be made, in the old stories incomprehensibly mine, to find his, it must be there somewhere, it must have been mine, before being his, I'll recognise it, in the end I'll recognise it, the story of the silence that he never left, that I should never have left, that I may never find again, that I may find again, then it will be he, it will be I, it will be the place, the silence, the end, the beginning, the beginning again, how can I say it, that's all words, they're all I have, and not many of them, the words fail, the voice fails, so be it, I know that well, it will be the silence, full of murmurs, distant cries, the usual silence, spent listening, spent waiting,

waiting for the voice, the cries abate, like all cries, that is to say they stop, the murmurs cease, they give up, the voice begins again, it begins trying again, quick now before there is none left, no voice left, nothing left but the core of murmurs, distant cries, quick now and try again, with the words that remain, try what, I don't know, I've forgotten, it doesn't matter, I never knew, to have them carry me into my story, the words that remain, my old story, which I've forgotten, far from here, through the noise, through the door, into the silence, that must be it, it's too late, perhaps it's too late, perhaps they have, how would I know, in the silence you don't know, perhaps it's the door, perhaps I'm at the door, that would surprise me, perhaps it's I, perhaps somewhere or other it was I, I can depart, all this time I've journeyed without knowing it, it's I now at the door, what door, what's a door doing here, it's the last words, the true last, or it's the murmurs, the murmurs are coming, I know that well, no, not even that, you talk of murmurs, distant cries, as long as you can talk, you talk of them before and you talk of them after, more lies, it will be the silence, the one that doesn't last, spent listening, spent waiting, for it to be broken, for the voice to break it, perhaps there's no other, I don't know, it's not worth having, that's all I know, it's not I, that's all I know, it's not mine, it's the only one I ever had, that's a lie, I must have had the other, the one that lasts, but it didn't last, I don't understand, that is to say it did, it still lasts, I'm still in it, I left myself behind in it, I'm waiting for me there, no, there you don't wait, you don't listen, I don't know, perhaps it's a dream, all a dream, that would surprise me, I'll wake, in the silence, and never sleep again, it will be I, or dream, dream again, dream of a silence, a dream silence, full of murmurs, I don't know, that's all words, never wake, all words, there's nothing else, you must go on, that's all I know, they're going to stop, I know that well, I can feel it, they're going to abandon me, it will be the silence, for a moment, a good few moments, or it will be mine, the lasting one, that didn't last, that still lasts, it will be I, you must go on, I can't go on, you must go on, I'll go on, you must say words, as long as there are any, until they find me, until they say me, strange pain, strange sin, you must go on, perhaps it's done already, perhaps they have said me already, perhaps they have carried me to the threshold of my story, before the door that opens on my story, that would surprise me, if it opens, it will be I, it will be the silence, where I am, I don't know, I'll never know, in the silence you don't know, you must go on, I can't go on, I'll go on.